D0375425

STORIES WITHOUT ENDINGS

PUSHING THE LIMITS

GLOBE FEARON EDUCATIONAL PUBLISHER
A Division of Simon & Schuster
Upper Saddle River, New Jersey

Project Editor: Lynn W. Kloss
Editorial Assistant: Kristen Shepos
Editorial Supervisor: Steven Otfinoski
Production Manager: Penny Gibson
Production Editor: Linda Greenberg
Marketing Manager: Sandra Hutchison
Interior Electronic Design and Art Supervision: Joan Jacobus
Electronic Page Production: José A. López
Illustrator: Allen Davis
Cover Design: Patricia Smythe
Cover Illustration: © Jerry McDaniel '94

Printed in the United States of America.
  2 3 4 5 6 7 8 9 10 99 98 97 96

ISBN: 0-835-91214-0

Globe Fearon Educational Publisher
A Division of Simon & Schuster
Upper Saddle River, New Jersey

Contents

About This Book

This book can be an adventure. Within its pages are people who must decide whether to join gangs, betray a friend, take a chance on love, or even risk their lives.

The best part, though, is the ending that you write. In most stories, the author decides what happens. In these stories, you decide whether the characters will do the right thing or take the easy way out. It's in your hands.

As you read these stories, think about how you might handle the situations. Think about what others you know might do if faced with that problem. You might also consider a completely new solution. Use your imagination to find the perfect, unexpected ending.

As you think about the ending you'll write, though, remember that you're writing for characters in a story, not for yourself. Try to make the decision you think the character might make.

Some of these characters may face unpleasant situations you recognize. If the plot of one story makes you uncomfortable, you might want to finish another one instead. It is possible, though, that thinking about the situation the character faces may provide you with some new ways of dealing with problems in your life.

You can also find ways to finish these stories by talking over the situation with friends, parents, or brothers and sisters. Play the scene out in your mind and "see" what might happen next. You could try different endings to see which one works best. You might also get together with a friend and read the story aloud, trying out different endings.

Above all, have fun. Relax and let your imagination take over. You might even surprise yourself.

A New Friend

by Cynthia Benjamin

Have you ever moved to a new neighborhood? About a month ago, I did. Right now, I'm a little confused. Part of me feels great. Part of me feels pretty weird. Let me explain.

First, I'll tell you about the great part. My family finally moved to a new apartment this summer. My mom got a terrific job. My 10-year-old sister Shauna is definitely acting more normally in public. When we go to restaurants, I don't feel so embarrassed that I pretend she's with another family. OK, so I still don't like having to share a bedroom with her. But this time it's a big bedroom. We each have our own closet, and I took the bed nearest the window. When I open it wide, I can actually look out and see the sky. That's a big improvement over our old apartment. When I opened a window there, I looked into someone else's apartment.

Then there's our neighborhood. (Remember: I'm still on the great part of my story.) It's clean. It's safe. I felt at home the minute I saw it. A couple of the kids from my new school live in my building. I met two of them in the laundry room a few weeks ago. Usually, I'm kind of shy. No, that's not quite right. Usually, meeting new kids makes my stomach turn into a ball. I'm not talking about a Ping-Pong ball or even a baseball. I'm talking about a beach ball that gets bigger and bigger as I get more and more nervous. But since we moved, I haven't felt like that. Maybe it has something to do with turning 15. Maybe it has something to do with moving to a new place.

All I know is that I felt fine talking to Lynn and Keema.

As it turns out, they live on the same floor in my building. They've been friends, like, forever. But they were really nice to me. Keema thought we'd probably be in the same home-room. She and Lynn even offered to show me around the school. When I brought our laundry back to the apartment, I couldn't wait to tell my mom.

While Mom and I were folding the sheets and towels, I told her all about my new friends. "Charlene," she said, "I'm really proud of you. I know you were worried about moving to a new neighborhood. But you're making a good start. They sound like very nice girls."

I continued folding the laundry. Mom looked so pleased that I decided not to tell her that Shauna had left her red crayon in her jeans pocket again. It had sort of dissolved in the washing machine.

Mom was right about Lynn and Keema. They *were* nice. In fact, they turned out to be really amazing. Also, they were friends with other amazing kids. Everyone in school looked up to their crowd. Being friends with them meant that maybe I could be a part of the crowd, too.

I admit the first day of school was pretty scary. But Lynn and Keema showed me around. They even introduced me to their friends. I couldn't believe it.

At my old school, in my old life, I was always kind of out of things. You know what I mean. I was one of the nerds who doesn't even know when the clothes styles change. The nerds sat together at the same lunch table, the one closest to the kitchen. By the middle of the semester, every-one just called it the "nerd table." I was too shy to move anywhere else.

Well, things sure changed. My nerd image was yester-day's news. Then I met Denise Hartley. That's when life changed from being great to being kind of confused.

It started the third day of school. Denise was a transfer student, too. She had arrived a few days late because her family had just moved from Texas. Our guidance counselor, Mr. Rodriguez, thought it was a good idea for Denise and me to meet. He figured we had a lot in common. Let me tell you something. He figured wrong.

I first saw Denise in Mr. Rodriguez's office. All I could think was, "Boy, she looks familiar." Denise was about my height and weight. She wore big, round glasses. Her hair was kind of wild, and her clothes were kind of nerdy. All of a sudden it hit me. The reason Denise looked so familiar was that she looked just like I did in the old days. I had traded in my glasses for contacts. After hanging out with Lynn and Keema, I had changed my hair style, too. I was still working on my clothes. But I was learning fast. In a few more weeks, I might even manage to look like everyone else—I mean, the really "in" group. I definitely didn't want to look like Denise Hartley anymore—and I definitely didn't want to hang out with her.

There was just one problem. It started in Mr. Rodriguez's office. He gave me and Denise this huge, guidance counselor kind of smile. Then he said the fateful words. "Charlene, you seem to be settling in just fine. I thought you might enjoy showing Denise around school."

What could I say? How could I possibly explain that I didn't want to be seen with someone who looked like the old me? All I wanted was to fit in. The new Charlene Norris

was definitely a blender. Now I was stuck with someone who looked like the "before" picture in an article about makeup makeovers. But that's not the worst part. The worst part happened about a week later.

In a week, I had learned a lot about Denise. She turned out to be a major brain. OK, I have to admit that I'm smart, too, but I try not to show it too much. I figure that way I fit in better. But Denise didn't see it that way. She didn't act smart to show off. Denise really liked to think and talk about ideas. When I was with Keema or Lynn, we mostly talked about how we looked and how the other girls looked. The rest of the time, we talked about the guys in our class and how they looked. Pretty deep, right?

With Denise it was different. For one thing, she didn't care about clothes. I'd point out a terrific pair of jeans—I couldn't wait to try them on. But all Denise said was, "Charlene, it's only a pair of jeans." If I suggested that she try to dress like the other kids in our school, Denise just shrugged. "I don't care about that. The only person I want to look like is me."

At first, I had a hard time figuring Denise out. I thought she was living in another world or something. But my mother thought Denise was living in her own world. "I think your friend just wants to be her own person, Charlene," she said. "You have to respect her for that."

You know something? That's exactly what happened. Remember that I said there was a part of my story that made me feel weird and confused? Well, that has something to do with the worst thing that happened. First, I spent about a week or so trying to avoid her. When she walked into the lunchroom, I waited until she sat down at a table. After the table filled up, I walked in to buy my lunch. That way I could sit where I wanted to—at Lynn and Keema's table. Now, I'm not very proud of the way I acted. But that's still not the worst thing that happened.

The worst thing is that the more I got to know Denise, the more I liked her. I knew she wasn't like the really "in" kids. But after awhile, I stopped caring about that stuff. Denise was interested in lots of things, like photography and old movies. She had set up a darkroom in her basement. She even offered to teach me how to develop my next roll of film. Hanging out with her turned out to be more interesting than being with Lynn and Keema. That was part of my problem. I liked being friends with Denise. But part of me still wanted to be seen with the really "in" kids. The more time I spend with Denise, the less time Keema and Lynn want to spend with me.

It didn't take long to recognize the signs. When Denise answered a question in class, Lynn and Keema looked at each other and rolled their eyes. The more she talked, the more annoyed they looked. Keema and Lynn were giving her "the treatment." The other kids in our class saw it, too. Even our history teacher, Ms. Epstein, saw it. There was only one person who didn't seem to notice what was happening—Denise.

It got worse, too. By this time, I was eating lunch with Denise practically every day. About a week ago, we walked into the lunchroom late. Nearly all the seats were taken. There were two seats, but they were at Keema's table. When Denise and I tried to sit down, Keema covered them with her backpack. "Sorry, guys," she said, "these are saved. I think there's room at that table over there." She pointed in the direction of the nerds' table. It was next to the kitchen.

Denise and I walked home from school that afternoon. When I tried to talk about what had happened, she cut me off. "Those guys don't bother me," she said. For a minute, she looked sad. Then her face brightened. "Hey, don't forget about Friday night." She was going to help me develop my pictures. I was looking forward to it.

I was walking across the lobby of my apartment building when I saw Keema and Lynn standing next to the elevator. As soon as they saw me, they stopped talking. For the first time in months, my stomach started to ball up. I know I should have been angry about what they did at lunch, but all I wanted to do was avoid fighting with them. If they turned against me, I would never be able to hang out with any of the kids in their crowd again.

"Hey, Charlene," Keema said. "Where have you been keeping yourself?" I couldn't believe it. They knew exactly where I'd been. Of course, I decided not to let on.

"I'm having a party this weekend," Lynn said. "Friday night, around 8:00. Why don't you come over?"

My heart started to pound. I had heard about Keema and Lynn's parties. If you were invited to one, you were part of their crowd, and they had just invited me.

Then I remembered Denise. How could I go to the party when I was supposed to hang out with her on Friday? "OK," I said to myself. "Maybe it's not so bad. Maybe you can bring Denise to the party."

Then Keema and Lynn exchanged looks. "There's just one thing," Lynn said. I knew what was coming. "We like you. But Denise is kind of strange. You're still new in school and you should be making friends, *other* friends."

Keema gave me a big smile. "That's why coming to this party would be so good for you. I hope you can make it." Then they waved and left me standing there in the lobby.

Well, it's Friday night. The party starts in about an hour. That's exactly when I'm supposed to be at Denise's house. Didn't I say I felt confused? Now, I've been thinking about this all week, and I know what I'm going to do. I'm going to call . . .

IIII■*THINKING ABOUT THE STORY*

1. Describe what Charlene was like before she moved to her new apartment.

2. How does Charlene think she's changed since she moved?

3. Why do you think it's so important to Charlene to be accepted by Keema and Lynn?

4. How is Denise Hartley different from Keema and Lynn?

5. What does Charlene's mother mean when she says that Denise "wants to be her own person"?

6. How do Charlene's feelings about Denise change as she gets to know her?

IIII▉ THINKING ABOUT THE ENDING

Charlene is having conflicting feelings about her friendship with Denise and her need to be accepted by Lynn, Keema, and their friends. Think about what you have learned about the characters. Think also about how Charlene feels about herself.

Do you think Charlene will go to Lynn's party? Why or why not? Write an ending for the story in which Charlene makes her choice. Remember to write your ending in the first person, as if Charlene is talking directly to the reader.

Is There a Doctor in the House?

by Kipp Erante Cheng

The best time of the year for Jordan Wu was the summertime. He could sleep as late as he wanted, eat whatever snacks his mother bought, and watch every single game show on television.

During the school year, Jordan missed a lot of his favorite game shows. When he got back home, his parents made him do all his homework before he could watch the videotapes of the shows he had recorded that day.

When Jordan came home from school one fateful day and announced that he would not be following in the footsteps of his mother or his father or even his older brother and sister, the entire family was shocked.

"Family, I have an announcement to make," Jordan said hesitantly. "I have decided not to become a doctor. Instead, I want to be a game show host."

The room was deadly quiet. Jordan's mother and father were silent, while his older brother and sister just sat and stared at him. Finally, Jordan's father broke the silence.

"Are you sure this is the decision you want to make, Jordan?" Dr. Wu asked. "Don't you want to be a doctor like everyone else in our family?"

"No," Jordan replied, "that's not where my heart is. I want to be in the entertainment business. I want to rub elbows with famous and important people. I want to have my own personal fan club."

His mother cut in. "Some doctors have fan clubs of their own, too, you know."

"Like which doctors?" Jordan asked.

The family was stumped to think of a doctor with a fan club.

"I want to do something different with my life, " Jordan said. "Can't you understand that?"

No one knew what to say to that.

There were only a few days of summer left before school began. These days were always the most precious to Jordan. Each year, he tried to draw out each moment of each day and make the most of it. With a bowl of popcorn in front of him, the remote control in his hand, and the television program guide flipped to the listings of game shows, Jordan watched television. He dreamed of growing up and becoming a famous game show host. Maybe one day he would host a show like *The Price Is Right* or even a more intellectual show like *Jeopardy!* In either case, Jordan was determined to be in the spotlight. All he had to do to accomplish his goal was to finish high school, go to college, and then start to audition for parts on game shows.

"I know I would be a great game show host," Jordan said out loud to himself, later that evening.

"You think so?" Dr. Wu said.

"How long have you been standing there, Dad?" Jordan said, a little surprised.

"Long enough to hear what you said," Dr. Wu said. "You like watching game shows, Son?"

"No, not really," Jordan said.

"No?" Dr. Wu said.

"No, I don't *like* watching games shows, I *love* watching game shows," Jordan said, smiling at his father.

"Why do you love to watch them?" Dr. Wu asked.

"I don't know. I can't really explain why," admitted Jordan. "I think they're fun. I like to imagine that everyone on the show could be a winner. After they win, they go home and tell all their friends they were on television. I think that would be great. I like the idea of becoming rich and famous, but I also like the idea of entertaining people."

"I see," Dr. Wu said.

"Hey, Dad," Jordan said. "Did you always want to be a doctor?"

"No," Dr. Wu said, laughing. "When I was your age, I wanted to be a pilot."

"Really?"

"Sure. When I was a child, I wanted to grow up and fly airplanes. I wanted to travel around the world and meet interesting people and see different things."

"Then why did you become a doctor?" Jordan asked, confused.

"Going back four generations, there have been doctors in this family. Your grandfather was a doctor and his father, too. There was a lot of pressure on me to uphold the family tradition," Dr. Wu said.

"Do you regret becoming a doctor and not following your dream?" asked Jordan.

"Sometimes," Dr. Wu said. "I sometimes wonder what my life would have been like if I hadn't gone to medical school. But that feeling doesn't last very long. If I hadn't gone to medical school, I wouldn't have met your mother, and if I hadn't met your mother, I wouldn't have this family, a family that I am very proud to have."

"I see," Jordan said, not quite sure what else to say. "School starts next week."

"You'll be in the tenth grade. Time sure passes by very quickly," Dr. Wu said. "I can remember when you were in diapers."

"Dad! That was so long ago," Jordan said, slightly embarrassed.

"You're right, Son," Dr. Wu said. "You're our youngest child. I just wanted to let you know that your mother and I will support whatever decision you make."

"Thanks, Dad," Jordan said.

Jordan felt better after talking with his father. However, he also felt as if he had learned something about his father. His father had never talked about wanting to be a pilot. Jordan always assumed that his father and his mother wanted to be doctors all their lives.

Jordan decided to ask his mother the same question he had asked his father.

"Of course not," his mother said. "Becoming a doctor was the last thing on my mind."

"Really?" Jordan said.

"I thought I was going to grow up and become a concert pianist or a dancer," she said. "The last thing I thought I would become was a doctor."

"I'm surprised to hear that, Mom."

"Why are you so surprised, Jordan?"

"I mean, I grew up assuming that everyone who was in a Chinese-American family became a doctor. Now you and Dad tell me that you had other plans when you were younger. It kind of freaks me out."

His mother laughed. "Listen, Jordan, when you're young, you get to do a lot of different things. Your father and I want you to try as many different things as you can. But when you grow up, you have to make a decision about what you want to do for the rest of your life. When that day comes, your family will support you whether or not you want to be a doctor or a pilot or a lawyer or—"

"A game show host?" Jordan asked.

"Yes, even a game show host," his mother said.

"Thanks, Mom," Jordan said.

That night, Jordan had a dream. He dreamed that he was sitting at home, watching *The Wheel of Fortune*. Vanna White had just turned the letter *E*. As Jordan watched Vanna walk across the stage turning letter after letter, he suddenly realized that he was the contestant who had bought the vowel. Jordan was no longer in the living room of his parents' house, but was standing in the studio of *The Wheel of Fortune*, buying vowels and chatting with Pat Sajak and Vanna White.

"Tell us a little about yourself, Jordan," Pat Sajak asked.

"Well, Pat . . ." Jordan felt tongue-tied.

"Come on, Jordan," Vanna chimed in. "Cat got your tongue?"

The entire studio audience burst out into laughter.

"I . . ." Jordan tried to speak once again. "I'm a high school student and when I grow up . . ."

"Yes?" Pat asked with anticipation.

"When I grow up, I want to become a doctor, like my father and my mother and my brother and sister." Jordan was both horrified and relieved to have said that on national television.

"That sounds like an excellent career choice, Jordan," Pat said. "The world could always use a talented doctor."

"Yes, the world needs more doctors," Vanna said. "I need one myself."

Again, the audience burst into wild laughter.

Jordan didn't know what to do. He knew that this was all a dream, but why did he tell Pat Sajak and the rest of the nation that we was going to be a doctor?

"Is there a doctor in the house?" Vanna asked. The audience began to laugh so hard that some people actually fell out of their seats.

"I think Vanna's serious about this one," Pat Sajak said.

Sure enough, Jordan stood at the giant wheel of fortune and watched as Vanna clutched her stomach and collapsed, right in front of his eyes. Jordan jumped across the wheel and hopped onto the stage, where Vanna was breathing heavily.

"Is there a doctor in the house?" Vanna gasped.

"Do your job, Jordan!" Pat Sajak said, sounding very worried.

Jordan took out a magic medical bag and searched inside for a potion that would save Vanna's life. He found what he was looking for and gave her the medicine. Suddenly, she jumped to her feet fully recovered.

"This young man has saved my life!" Vanna said, looking radiant.

"I'm proud of you, Jordan!" Pat Sajak said. "You will make an excellent doctor one day!"

Then in a flash, Jordan woke up to find himself in bed. He went into the bathroom and looked at himself in the mirror. There was something different about the way his face looked. He felt older and wiser. He felt as if there was a change on the inside that showed on the outside. But what could his dream have meant? He tried to forget about it and shake off the idea of becoming a doctor. He reminded himself about the spotlight and the fame and his own personal fan club. Jordan tried to weigh the differences between being a game show host and being a doctor. He wanted to be rich and famous, but he also liked the feeling of helping people. He thought about his dream, and he thought about his future. Finally, he came to a decision.

Later that morning, Jordan went to the kitchen to get his breakfast. Although there were a few days left of summer vacation, Jordan woke up early to talk to his mother and father before they went to the hospital.

"Jordan, you're up early for a summer day," his mother said.

"I have an important announcement to make," Jordan said.

"What is it, Son?" his father asked.

Jordan took a deep breath. "I've decided that I will . . .

||||■ THINKING ABOUT THE STORY

1. What kinds of expectations does Jordan's family have for him?
2. What kinds of expectations does Jordan have of his family?

3. Why does Jordan want to be a game show host when he grows up?

4. How do Jordan's conversations with his father and mother affect his opinion of them?

5. Describe Jordan's dream.

THINKING ABOUT THE ENDING

Jordan comes from a family of doctors. Although they expect him to follow in the Wu family footsteps, Jordan's parents want him to make his own decisions. Jordan becomes confused about his future after his dream. What are some of his thoughts about a career in medicine and a career as a game show host? Write an ending that tells which career he chooses and how that choice affects his life.

Magda

by Chiori Santiago

The sun, which was just beginning to burn over the desert, slanted through the curtains. It touched the foot of Magda's bed and then crept toward her head, waking her gently. The best mornings began this way, Magda thought as she stretched under the covers. Summer was great, she decided. No jangling alarm clock. No rushing to classes. Just her night job at Casey's Fast Food Shack and the rest of the day to be lazy. Work at Casey's was easy— cleaning the grill, making milkshakes, and joking around with the regulars while she swept the floor.

She knew everyone in town, so working at Casey's was like hanging around with family. There were the regulars the Friday-night-out couples, Mrs. Ross with her six kids, and old Byron, who always ordered the same thing— cheeseburger rare. Casey's was right near the border fence that separated Magda's town of Saint Mary from the Mexican town of Santa María, just on the other side. So besides the regulars at the Fast Food Shack, there were always truckers and tourists and families from Mexico, going back and forth after shopping in each other's country on a day pass. It was a busy place. Magda liked it that way.

"Maggie, another cup of coffee, when you get to it," Red Don, one of the truckers would say and then leave a big tip. "For your college fund, babe," he'd say on the way out.

Everyone at Casey's knew about Magda's college fund. She'd been talking about it since she started working there in tenth grade. Casey, the owner of the Fast Food Shack, used to be a trucker himself, and he loved to tell stories of the road. He'd talk about the time he broke down in Texas and a preacher came along, laid his hands on the hood of the truck, and got it running again. Or the town in Arizona where the houses were made out of boulders, like in *The Flintstones*. Casey had eaten roasted alligator tail in Louisiana and spent the night under a giant cement dinosaur in Nebraska.

Magda wanted to see those places, too. Much as she loved her hometown, there was no future here in Saint Mary. If she stayed, she'd end up working at Casey's forever, like Dahlia, who'd started frying hamburgers in high school and who was still behind the counter. Dahlia was happy, but Magda wanted more. When Casey hired her last year, he asked what she was going to do with her paycheck. "I'm getting out of this border town and going to school," she'd said firmly. "I'm going to get a diploma, go to college back East somewhere, travel, and see snow."

The dollar bills and dimes and quarters that folks left in her tip jar really couldn't pay for college. But Magda worked as hard in school as she did at Casey's. She was one of ten students in her school chosen for a state scholarship. The scholarship would pay tuition for one year to the state college in Blue Bluff. If she got good grades, she could apply for an extension the next year.

"Well, it's not back East, but it's a start," she told Casey the day she got the news.

"You bet, honey," said Casey. "Don't forget to clean the grease pan under the grill, OK? Now don't give me that face. Whatever happens in life, it's good to know how to clean a grease pan. It may come in handy someday."

"Yeah, right, Casey," said Magda, grinning. That was Casey's way of saying "Good luck—we'll miss you."

Of course, she still had to get through senior year, but she wasn't worried. The hard stuff was over. Senior year would be a breeze, she thought. No, the hard part would be solving the Big Problem, the one she didn't want to think about.

Magda shuffled into her slippers and walked, yawning, into the kitchen. In the summer, it was her job to do the dishes and straighten the house after her mother left for work. The minute she stepped into the kitchen, the Big Problem hit her in the face.

There were four plates on the table and four coffee cups. Magda and her mother lived alone, and she hadn't heard any noise last night. No doors slamming, no hellos that would mean family had come to visit. Whoever had eaten the quesadillas and toast and drunk the coffee had done so in silence, early this morning, before Magda was awake. They didn't want to wake her. Magda knew why.

She sighed as she cleared away the tortillas—which by now were as hard as hockey pucks. She was worried. She'd been worried ever since she found out who the night visitors were.

Sometime in the past few months, the night visitors had begun to come. She would find traces of them, as she did this morning. The leftovers she'd packed carefully into the refrigerator the night before would be gone. Once an old pair of sneakers she was planning to throw out disappeared from the back porch. Then one Saturday, she came into the kitchen early and saw a small, dark man sitting at the table with her mother. They looked up, surprised.

"Oh, Magda," said her mother. "This is—Señor Angel. He's just arrived to help the caretaker at the church." But when the man spoke, his Spanish sounded funny. It wasn't Mexican Spanish, and his clothes looked odd. He wasn't born in Saint Mary, Magda thought, or even in Santa María. What was going on?

That night, she asked. "Who was he, Mom? What are you hiding?"

Her mother sat down and looked at her hands. "Magdalena, listen to me," she said. "I'll tell you what's going on, but you have to keep it to yourself." She looked up. "OK?"

Magda nodded. She expected the worst.

"You know the kind of work I do at the church," her mother said. Magda nodded again. Her mother was secretary and bookkeeper at St. Mary's Catholic Church, the biggest church in town. She also helped with clothing drives, pancake breakfasts, the Christmas toy donations, and other projects at the church. Sometimes Magda helped. Every Christmas season, Magda and her mother would drive across the border with boxes of donated toys from the church for the kids in Santa María. Magda liked to see the smiles on the kids' faces when she handed out the toys.

"Well, Magda, we've gotten involved in some other work for a good cause," her mother said slowly. "You know about the wars, don't you?"

"What wars?" said Magda.

"In Central America," her mother explained. "They're fighting everywhere—in Guatemala, in El Salvador. Good people, innocent people—farmers and people in the coun-tryside, people who are just trying to make a living—get caught in the middle."

"What does that have to do with us?" Magda asked.

"The point is that people are escaping north," her moth-er said. "Some of them have lost their whole families. They're leaving and coming across Mexico, and they end up here."

"OK. So?"

"So the church is helping them find food, clothing, and shelter."

Magda let out a sigh of relief. "So that's what old Señor Angel was doing here? Thank goodness!"

"Oh, Magda, I'm so glad you understand." Her mother stood up.

"But what's the big secret?" Magda asked. "Why do you have to bring them home? Can't they just go to the Red Cross or something, or eat at the church?"

Magda's mother sat down again. "Magda, they can't. They're—illegals. They come through a hole in the border fence at night, and they find their way here. If the Immigration Service finds them, they'll be sent back."

Now it was Magda's turn to jump up. "Illegals! Mom! Don't you know what this means?" Thoughts of the scholarship leaped into her head. The scholarship was from the state. When she was chosen for the scholarship, she'd signed papers to promise she wouldn't damage school property or be in a protest march or take part in "un-American activities." One thing was certain—helping illegal immigrants had to be an un-American activity. There were people in her own house who were breaking the law! If the state found out, they might take away her scholarship.

"Mom, this is crazy," Magda went on. "There's a limit to what you have to do for the church. What if you get caught? If the illegals get caught, they're just sent back. But you— what if you got arrested?"

She could see tears in her mother's eyes. "Magda, sweetheart, if these people are sent back to Guatemala or El Salvador, they could die. One woman came to us all alone. The soldiers killed her two sons. They were only teenagers. You wouldn't believe the horror stories. I'm part of a group of people helping to get these people protection—asylum, it's called. It's a risk, but it's worth it. I can't stand by and do nothing."

"Oh, Mom." Magda reached out and patted her mother's back. It was true. Her mother could never stand by when someone needed help. But sometimes Magda wished her mother would stop helping other people and pay attention to her own child. Magda thought of all the times she'd been left alone on weekends because her mother was busy giving out food in Santa María or going door to door asking for donations.

"I wish you'd care about me the way you care about them," Magda blurted out.

"What?"

Magda couldn't stop herself. "You know, all I've wanted for years has been a chance to go to college, and now you could ruin it. What if the immigration people came here? You know how they watch the border. What if someone reported us? I could lose my scholarship. I've worked hard to earn it, Mom. You know I have. Think about me for a change. I'm your daughter!"

Magda's mother pushed her away. "I can't believe it," she said, in a voice that made Magda want to cry. "I can't believe I raised a child who is so selfish."

As she cleared the dishes, Magda could see nothing had changed. The Big Problem was still there. She wondered what to do. If any illegals showed up while she was here, perhaps the best thing to do was to turn them in herself. That would prove that she wasn't part of any illegal activity, and maybe she could keep the scholarship. The immigration officers would come and pick up the illegals and drive them to the border. The immigrants would find someone else to help them, maybe in Mexico or in another house in Saint Mary, and Magda could go on with her future.

On the other hand, wouldn't she get her mother in trouble? She couldn't do that. Of course she wasn't that selfish. But maybe the church would protect her mom and see that she didn't go to jail. Magda didn't want to think about the people escaping the war. Would they really be shot if they went back, as her mother had said? How could she know that? Maybe it was just a tall tale.

Magda thought she heard the back door rattle. Everything's getting to me nowadays, she thought. No, there it was—a knock, soft and timid. She stepped to the back door and opened it wide.

She stared at the woman who stood on the back porch. The woman was shorter than Magda and coffee-skinned. She was barefoot. Her hair was in braids, and she wore a long skirt of bright colors that glowed beneath a layer of dust. Oh, no, thought Magda, she's one of them. The woman held a small boy by the hand. The boy was barefoot, too. His feet were covered with sores and his face was dirty.

"*Discúlpeme, por favor,*" the woman said in careful Spanish, her eyes frightened and sad. "*Puede ayudarme, gracias a Dios?*"

Can you help me, with God's grace? Magda stared at the woman. The phone was just a few steps away in the kitchen. If she walked over and picked it up, she could easily dial the immigration office and separate herself from this whole business. She looked at the little boy, who was rubbing his eyes, leaving a streak of dust across his face. He didn't smile. Magda closed her eyes to think, one hand on the doorknob. Then she . . .

||||| THINKING ABOUT THE STORY

1. What kind of place is Casey's, and why is Magda happy working at Casey's?
2. Why do you think Magda wants to leave her home town?
3. Should Magda's mother take risks to help people from another country? Is it really her responsibility?

4. How does Magda feel about her mother's charity?

5. Is it selfish of Magda to want to go to college?

IIIITHINKING ABOUT THE ENDING

Magda is caught in the middle of a difficult decision. If she helps her mother, she could be breaking the law and may lose her scholarship. If she doesn't help her mother, she will be turning her back on people in need. Is there a right choice in this situation?

Using what you know about Magda's dreams and her values, write an ending to the story that tells the choice she makes.

*F*inal Inning

by Gerald Tomlinson

I darted to my left, fielded the hard grounder cleanly, and fired the ball across the infield to our first baseman.

"Out!" barked the umpire.

That was the 13th batter in a row that our Falcon pitcher, Marv Gilson, had gotten out. Marv had a no-hit, no-run game going. We led 2–0, and Marv looked unbeatable.

I was the Falcon shortstop. I'd driven in both our runs with a second-inning homer over the left-field fence. Still, the hero of the game was clearly Marv, and Marv would have been the first to say so.

"I'm the best pitcher in the Southside Conference," Marv told the team at the beginning of the season. "Get me a run or two, and we'll win every game."

I'll admit Marv was good. Our team had won eight games and lost two with Gilson on the mound. A win today, and we'd be conference champions.

Yes, Marv was our ace, but he had a tremendous ego. When I hit my second-inning home run, he never said a word to me. He never even looked at me. The other players gave me the high five, but Marv just sat there on the bench with a self-satisfied grin, as if it were *his* game, not mine nor anyone else's.

The parents and students in the stands were on Marv's side. It's true that they cheered when I hit my homer. But they cheered just as wildly every time Marv threw a strike. After the top of the fourth inning, having set down 12 batters in a row, Marv actually tipped his hat to the crowd as he headed toward the bench. Talk about showing off!

You might have figured out by now that I didn't like Marv Gilson. I never had. The other players on the Falcons played as a team, but not Marv. He always had to be the main attraction, the star of the show.

Now here he was, pitching a perfect game against Wilson High. It was not just a no-hitter, but an absolutely perfect game—no walks, no errors, no wild pitches, no hit batters.

The 14th Wilson batter hit an easy fly ball to our left fielder. Next up was Roscoe Jones, Wilson's big, strong catcher and one of their best hitters. Last time up, Jones had sent our center fielder to the fence to haul down a screaming line drive.

Marv Gilson looked as confident as ever. He burned a strike past Jones and then tried a curve ball. Marv's curve fooled a lot of batters, but it didn't fool Roscoe Jones.

Jones swung hard and slashed the ball on the ground between the third baseman and me. We were both playing deep. Without thinking, I dove to my left and trapped the ball. Jones was a fast runner. It would take a perfect throw to get him at first. I scrambled up, set quickly, and threw hard.

The throw was low. It raised a puff of dust about 2 feet in front of Jeff Robinson, our first basemen. Jeff scooped it up like a pro, and the umpire snapped, "Out!"

The crowd cheered wildly, and I heard a few shouts of "Way to go, Larry" and "Way to go, Jeff." There were also a few cries of "Keep it up, Marv" and "You got 'em, Marv."

Marv didn't tip his hat this time. Neither did he say a word to Jeff or me. He just sat down on the bench and watched the Wilson pitcher take his warm-ups.

In the last of the fifth inning, we threatened to break the game open. The first two Falcon batters singled, and the third drew a walk, loading the bases with no one out. But then Jeff Robinson popped out to the second baseman, and the next batter took a called third strike. With two outs and the bases still loaded, I came to bat.

The excited crowd yelled for a hit. "Go get 'em, Larry," they cried. "Over the wall again, kid."

I wasn't trying for a home run. I'd have been happy to get a scratch single, anything to bring home at least one of those runners.

The Wilson pitcher was Al McCann, a tall guy with glasses and plenty of savvy. He caught me looking at a fast ball on the inside corner for strike one.

I stepped out of the batter's box, glanced down for the sign from the third base coach, kicked dirt from my spikes, and strode back in. McCann blazed a low pitch down the middle. I fouled it back for strike two.

The pitcher had me where he wanted me—0 and 2. But I was determined to get a hit. I swung late on McCann's next fastball and lined it down the right field line. The crowd roared and rose to its feet. When the ball sliced foul, they groaned and sat down.

McCann's next pitch missed the outside corner by a couple of inches. I stepped out. To my amazement, the umpire bellowed, "Strike three!"

I glanced back. Our coach insisted that we never argue strike calls, and I didn't. Instead, I stared coldly at the umpire until he turned away. He knew he'd called it wrong.

As I stood there, Marv Gilson trotted onto the field. Passing me, he said, "You could've clinched it for us right there, Larry. Choke, choke."

I couldn't believe it. Hadn't he seen my line-drive foul? Hadn't he spotted the bad call?

The top of the sixth inning passed quickly—one strikeout, one grounder to first base, and one fly ball to left field. Marv had to get only three more outs to achieve a perfect game.

We didn't score in the last of the sixth inning. That left it to Marv to finish up. He seemed eager to do so. Marv was as cocky as they come.

I was angry, really angry. We had our two-run lead because of my home run. I'd just missed a bases-clearing double or triple down the right-field line. Yet Marv had the nerve to say, "Choke, choke," when the umpire called me out on a bad pitch.

Going into the top of the seventh and last inning, I was willing to ruin Marv Gilson's perfect game if I got the chance. I knew I might get it. If a batter hit another hard grounder like Jones's between third and short, I could stab at it and deliberately miss the ball. The scorer would rule it a hit, ruining Marv's no-hitter and his perfect game. Even if the play was scored an error, Marv's perfect game would go up in smoke.

I thought about it. My desire to win was at least as strong as Marv Gilson's. Suppose that my intentional misplay led to a run? Or more than one run? What then? Would I still be happy to have put Marv in his place if we lost the game?

What about my teammates? They didn't like Marv either. Was anybody else thinking of bobbling a grounder or a fly? I didn't know, but I doubted it.

Still, Marv ought to realize how much his success depended not just on his pitching arm, but on the whole team. Even a better pitcher than Gilson couldn't strike out *everybody*, and as a hitter, Marv was a dud.

While I considered what to do about a hard grounder, the first Wilson batter fouled out to Jeff Robinson. Jeff made a nice play. He snatched the ball away from the hands of eager spectators in the front row behind first base.

That left two more Wilson hitters for Marv to retire. He got the first batter on a called third strike that was at least as far outside as the one that put me out.

With one out to go, my chances of affecting Gilson's perfect game were slim. Marv might strike out the last batter. Or, more likely, the ball might be hit to someone eager to make the last out in a perfect game.

Annoying as Marv was, he hadn't really angered anyone in this game except me, and he was pitching very well. Maybe he *did* deserve a perfect game.

The next Wilson batter was Jim Prather, a first baseman and a left-hander. Prather wasn't likely to hit the ball toward me. I breathed a sigh of relief. No moral decisions today.

Prather had a .380 batting average. He might have connected for a solid hit, ending the perfect game. But he didn't.

Although Marv had four different pitches, he seemed intent on erasing Prather with fast balls. To me, that wasn't a great idea. In our first game against Wilson, I'd seen the guy slam one of Marv's fast balls into left-center field for a triple.

Should I call time, walk over to Marv, and remind him that this guy could hit fast balls? Whether I should or not, I didn't.

On the next pitch, Prather pulled a Gilson fast ball high and deep toward right field. It had more than enough height and distance to clear the fence. But the ball kept hooking, hooking, hooking. At last, it sailed foul, landing far beyond the barrier. Strike.

I glanced toward Marv. His perfect game, no-hitter, and shutout had all come within inches of disappearing with that one tremendous clout. But Marv seemed as calm as ever. He just took the new ball from our catcher and prepared to throw again.

With the count at one ball and two strikes, he fired a pitch that fooled Prather completely. At the last second, the Wilson first baseman saw it would be a strike.

He poked desperately at the ball. He got a piece of it just off his hands and sent a weak fly toward left-center field. The outfielders were playing too deep to reach it. Neither the second baseman nor the third baseman had a chance to get there.

It was up to me. My chances weren't good. It would be a very tough play. The ball was just a low flare.

If I missed it, the scorer would call it a base hit. Thoughts of smug Marv Gilson raced through my mind as I watched the flight of the ball. Marv deserved a lesson, but was it right to miss the ball and possibly lose the game for the Falcons?

I raced back . . .

‖‖‖▪THINKING ABOUT THE STORY

1. Why does the narrator, Larry, dislike Marv Gilson?
2. Do you think Marv is as good a pitcher as he thinks he is? Why or why not?
3. How well does Larry play? How do you know?
4. Do you think that Larry should be as angry at Marv as he is? Explain.

5. Do you think Marv is more interested in winning or in pitching a perfect game?

6. Why does the perfect game depend on Larry, not the pitcher?

IIIII THINKING ABOUT THE ENDING

The narrator, Larry, can't stand Marv Gilson, the Falcon pitcher. He thinks that Marv sees himself as the only player on the team. Suddenly, he finds himself in a position to spoil Marv's perfect game.

Using what you know about Larry's feelings for Marv and his confusion about what to do, write a conclusion for this story. Describe Larry's thoughts as he runs for the ball, and the responses of the team and the crowd to his actions.

The Second Street Boys

by Cecilia Rubino

"Four sugars, OK, Victor?" Coco asked. He rubbed the stubble on his unshaven cheek and pulled a dollar out of his stained coat pocket.

"You got your Saturday all backwards, man," said Victor as he shook his head and smiled. "It's closing time and *now* you want coffee?"

Victor had arrived at Union Deli and Grocery at seven that morning. By eight, Coco had come in to exchange bottles and cans for a cold beer. Now, it was almost 11:00 P.M., and here he was back again for coffee.

"I don't know if you want this stuff." Victor peered into the coffee pot. "It's been sitting here all night," he said.

"I'm not picky; just make it light." Coco kept nervously rubbing his cheek and smoothing his unkempt hair. "Light, OK, Victor? A lot of milk. I need something extra in my stomach tonight."

The coffee had a thick, slightly burnt smell. Victor straightened his back as he poured. He was almost dizzy— that's how tired Victor felt. In fact, he'd needed some coffee himself in the past hour. It was the first time he'd worked a double shift. Mr. Choi's brother was taking a rare day off.

Union Deli and Grocery was a family business, but for as long as Victor could remember, Mr. Choi had hired kids from the neighborhood to help out. These days, it wasn't the only Korean market around. Lately, it seemed like there was one on every other block, but Victor's mom said Mr. Choi still had the best vegetables.

Most of what Victor did was grunt work—sweeping floors, working the deli counter, stocking shelves. But he didn't really mind. It felt good to be working. It was better than hanging around the house after school or playing stickball all weekend with the guys on Second Street. He'd just never put in so many hours before. No wonder he was exhausted. How did Mr. Choi do it every day?

"Got that coffee, Victor?" Coco asked again.

"Yeah, just getting some fresh milk." The hot liquid sizzled and spat as Victor poured it into the cup. "Let me make you a sandwich with this, man."

"I'm OK, had me a nice lunch earlier today," said Coco. "Ham, yellow rice, peaches, whipped cream. You got the sugars in there? Don't forget the sugars."

Coco couldn't stay still. He kept shifting his feet and restlessly pulling at his hair. He's high as a kite, Victor thought. Probably ate at the Soup Kitchen around the corner on Fourth Avenue, where they serve free lunch every day. Just before noon, dozens of homeless people regularly filed past Union Deli, walking or pushing their carts. They always stopped in for one thing or another. Mr. Choi wouldn't give credit the way the bodegas in the neighborhood did. But if somebody looked hungry, he let them take fruit, bread, or cupcakes. Junkies always wanted something sweet. Sugar. Sugar kept them going until their next score.

Victor heard Mr. Choi pulling down one of the metal gates outside. He pushed the lid on the cup and slipped it into a paper bag, along with the packets of sugar. He threw the last of the bread rolls in on top and handed the bag to Coco. "There you go, gotta close up now, OK?"

"I'm gone," said Coco, thrusting a crumpled dollar bill in Victor's direction.

Victor shook his head. "Don't worry about it man—bottom of the pot."

"You gotta nice boy there, Mr. C.," Coco said as Mr. Choi came in and joined Victor behind the register.

"I know, good boy, good worker," Mr. Choi patted Victor on the shoulder. *"Estamos cerrando; hasta mañana.* Closing up now; we'll see you tomorrow," he said to Coco in Spanish.

Victor didn't know how Mr. Choi did it. He not only spoke English, but he also spoke better Spanish than Victor. Victor's mom was always trying to get him to speak it at home. Although he understood what she was saying, he always answered back in English, so she had pretty much given up on him.

"Let's go, Coco," said Mr. Choi.

"He must be tired, too," Victor thought, as he stacked up crates of fruit to go down into the cooler.

"Just one more thing," Coco said and dropped the money on the counter. "Where are those hot, spicy things I like?"

"Barbecued chips? Right behind you," said Choi.

"Yeah, these are the best. You gotta taste these," Coco ripped open the bag, leaned across the counter to shove a chip into Mr. Choi's mouth. As Mr. Choi chewed politely, the ragged man quickly snatched a handful of disposable lighters from the counter and stuffed them into his pocket.

"Mañana, Coco, closing time," said the owner. Victor wasn't sure if Mr. Choi missed what had happened or was just letting it go. He began to walk Coco outside.

Coco knew all the tricks. Create a diversion, and then pick up whatever you can get your hands on. But Victor had kept his eye on him. He'd used the same tricks himself. One afternoon, when he'd been hanging out with the boys on Second Street, they'd gotten hungry, but they didn't have two dollars between them. So Louis ran his bike into the flower stand in front of Associated Grocery, while Victor and JoJo walked to the back of the store and loaded up their knapsacks with sodas and frozen pizzas.

Victor couldn't remember exactly how old he was when

he began to shoplift. He was pretty young, though. It had started back with the candy counter. It was so easy to reach out and pocket a handful, even with his mother standing right there. Then it just became a habit, a game. If something in a store caught his eye, he'd figure out a way to walk out with it. He had one of those blue coats with the fake fur around the hood for a couple of years. He'd made an extra pocket in the lining which he would fill up with all kinds of things: toys, comic books. He even took stuff that he didn't really want just because he couldn't stop himself. If his mom ever asked him where any of the things came from, he'd just say he was borrowing them from one of the boys on the block.

But he was never like some guys, bragging about what gangsters they were and showing off the stuff they stole. Even as a little kid, he didn't feel right about it and was always trying to stop.

Then he got caught. It was so stupid. He was with Louis and JoJo downtown, and all three of them tried to walk out of a department store with an extra pair of jeans on. The security guard was pretty nice about it, but they still called his mother and said they were putting it on his record. It was his mother who let him have it. "Is that how you want to end up?" she kept saying, "Nobody in this family has *ever* been to jail! Are you gonna be the first?"

That was six months ago. Afterwards, things on Second Street weren't the same. JoJo was still out there every day, playing stickball with the other guys. But Louis was off the block most of the time. Victor had his own problems. His mother wouldn't get off his back. But then his grades improved, and he got hired by Mr. Choi.

The guys really gave him a hard time when they heard about the job.

"You working for Mr. Chinese Man. How you like your chop suey?" JoJo teased.

"He's Korean," Victor corrected.

"Those guys don't like us," said JoJo.

"Get over it. He gave me a job!"

"Yeah, but what's he paying you?" Louis taunted, and the other guys answered together, "Chump change!"

The only time that he'd been back in good with them was the day he'd let Louis and JoJo walk out of Union Deli with an armful of beers. That night, it was like old home week on Second Street, but Victor told them it could never happen again. After that, they'd pretty much stopped talking to him.

Victor was proud that he'd never stolen anything from the deli himself, not even a can of soda. Mr. Choi liked him. He kept telling Victor that if he worked hard, some day he could open any kind of business he wanted. "People fresh off the boat must really believe that stuff," Victor thought. If you work hard, you can get your piece of the American pie. He was pretty sure that it didn't work like that for kids like him. How much money could he make with a business in this neighborhood, anyway?

But it made Victor think. What they really needed in the neighborhood was a sports store—a place with the right kind of shoes and designer equipment.

Victor was pulled out of his thoughts as he saw two guys with ski masks enter the store. One of them was shoving Mr. Choi back into the store from the street. Victor just stood there frozen, holding a crate of apples. The guy with the gun pointed to the register. Mr. Choi walked behind the counter and opened it up. "Here, take it," he said calmly. "We don't want any trouble here."

Then two shots went off. Victor saw the Korean man slump forward.

"Move it," said one of the two men. "Give us the money, now!" Victor recognized the voice. It was Louis! Both guys grabbed fistfuls of cash and ran out of the store. Victor dropped the apples and ran out after them. They were running toward Second Street.

A patrol car was cruising Fifth Avenue. Victor started waving his arms. He heard his own voice screaming.

"Officer, in here! He's been shot!" The car pulled up. One of the officers jumped out and headed for the store.

"Who did it?" the one in the driver's seat asked as he radioed for backup.

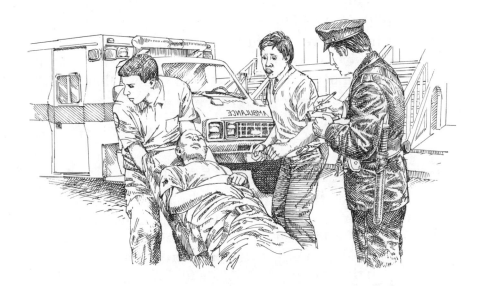

"Two kids! They went that way!" cried Victor.

"What'd they look like?"

Victor almost started to tell him and then froze up. How could he say it was Louis? He should keep his mouth shut. Should he rat on one of the Second Street boys? They would come looking for him if he did. "I don't know. They had ski masks on," Victor said.

When he saw Mr. Choi lifted into the ambulance, he was so choked up he couldn't talk. There was blood everywhere. They lifted him up on a stretcher. "Don't worry, Victor," said Mr. Choi. "It's gonna be OK. Don't worry. You lock up now."

"He'll be all right," one of the officers said. "He got hit in the shoulder; really lucky. Now, can you tell us what happened?"

Victor took a deep breath and . . .

IIII■ THINKING ABOUT THE STORY

1. Why does Victor shoplift?
2. Do you think getting caught changes him?
3. Why do the guys on Second Street tease Victor after he gets the job with Mr. Choi?
4. Mr. Choi believes that if you work hard, you can "get your piece of the American pie." Why does Victor think that only "people fresh off the boat believe that stuff"?
5. Why didn't Victor want to rat on Louis?

IIII■ THINKING ABOUT THE ENDING

Victor knows that his friend, Louis, is the one who shot Mr. Choi. Victor really cares about Mr. Choi. But he still has some feelings for his friends. Based on what you've learned about Victor, Mr. Choi, and the boys from Second Street, what do you think Victor will decide to do? Write an ending in which Victor decides whether or not to tell the cops and what happens as a result of his decision.

Tom Yellow Eagle's Friday Night

by James Bruchac

The alarm woke Tom Yellow Eagle from a deep sleep. He turned it off and lay there for a moment without moving. Rubbing his eyes, he slowly pulled off the covers. As he listened to the sound of the streets below, he sat up and placed his feet on the cold floor. "Another day of school," he said to himself as he walked out into the hallway to wake up his younger sisters.

Tom's mother had left for work hours ago. As his sisters dressed, Tom prepared their morning meal. Walking toward the cupboard, he paused and looked at the picture of his father on the wall. It had been almost ten years since his death. Tom looked closely at the picture, as he had many times before. His father's hair was long, like the Native Americans Tom had seen in the movies. Lately, he thought he noticed a resemblance to himself. As he studied the picture, his sisters walked into the room.

Tom had been only 6 when his father died, and his memories had faded. Still, he remembered his father's kindness and how he would take him on his lap when he got home from work. Often, his father would tell him stories, but Tom was too young to remember much of what they were about. Before his father's death, the whole family had lived on the reservation. They had attended powwows and other native gatherings. But they moved to the city shortly after his father's death, far away from any of their Native American relatives. His mother said it was because she needed to find work to support them now that "Daddy was gone."

Tom occasionally asked his mother questions about his Native American heritage. She would say, "We had hard times living on the reservation. Those are times we are better off forgetting. We have a new life now." She would often add, "You just stay in school, and you'll do fine. Let's leave the past behind us."

Tom's mother had to work two jobs and wasn't around much. More often than not, Tom was in bed before she got home, and she would be gone again before he and his sisters got up for school.

After breakfast, Tom and his sisters left the apartment and headed to school. As they walked, Tom's thoughts were still on his father. But as they turned the corner, Tom suddenly remembered—the school dance was tonight. His thoughts quickly focused on Cassandra, his date. Tom had had a crush on her for the last two years. A year before, Cassandra sat next to him in social studies. Tom thought about how they always talked and joked with each other before and after class.

Cassandra had a great sense of humor and was great to talk to. Tom had wanted to ask her out a hundred times but never had the courage. Even though they no longer had any classes together, Tom still stopped by Cassandra's locker to talk. She was always friendly, but Tom was never sure if she felt the way he did. A week ago, he decided he couldn't wait any longer, and he asked Cassandra to the dance. Tom smiled as he remembered walking up to Cassandra at her locker, his stomach in knots and his hands damp with nervous sweat.

Before he lost his confidence, he quickly said, "Cassandra, would you go to the dance with me next Friday?"

To his amazement, she said she'd love to go.

Tom arrived at school thinking about Cassandra. He hoped to have time enough to talk to her before first period.

Luckily, she was still at her locker when Tom arrived at school.

"Hi. Can I walk you to your class?" Tom asked, slightly out of breath from his run.

"That would be great," answered Cassandra.

They walked down the hallway toward Cassandra's classroom, talking mostly about classes and upcoming exams. Tom tried to hide his fears about the dance, but it was all he could think about. By the time they arrived at Cassandra's classroom, there was only a minute left before the bell rang.

"I'll see you at lunch," Tom said, heading toward his classroom.

"I'll save you a seat," Cassandra answered as Tom disappeared around the stairway. He made it to class just as the bell rang, pulling his books from his book bag as Mr. Brown, his history teacher, handed back yesterday's homework.

"Today, we have two visitors from the Black Ridge Indian Reservation," Mr. Brown said as moved across the room. "Let's move down to the auditorium."

On their way to the auditorium, Tom turned to a classmate and asked, "What reservation are these people from?"

"I think he said Black Ridge," answered the boy.

Tom felt a slight thrill as he realized Black Ridge was the reservation where he and his family had lived. "I wonder if these people knew our family?" he thought.

As the class entered the auditorium, Tom saw a Native American man and woman sitting on the stage. He sat down and looked closely at the two visitors. The man wore a black shirt with different-colored ribbons on it, like the one his father wore in the picture. The woman wore a leather dress with beautiful beadwork on the front and the sleeves.

When all the students were seated, the woman spoke. "Let's sit in a big circle," she said, pointing to the center of the auditorium.

Some of the students went to grab chairs.

"No chairs please. Everyone sit on the floor," the man said. Once all the students were seated, the woman spoke again.

"My name is Audrey Welch, and this is Matthew Deer. We are from the Black Ridge Reservation. We are here today to share a bit of our culture with you, through some of our stories and songs."

"Before we get started, let's go around the circle and have everyone tell their name," said Matthew Deer.

"My name is Tom Yellow Eagle," Tom said when it was his turn.

"Yellow Eagle? Any relation to Lance Yellow Eagle?" Matthew Deer asked.

"He was my father," Tom replied.

"I knew Lance very well," said Matthew Deer. "He was a good friend of mine and a great leader of our people. Let's talk after our performance."

As the rest of the students told their names, Tom sat there stunned. One of the performers actually knew the father he barely remembered! There were so many things he wanted to ask, so many questions his mother had never answered. Tom tried to focus on Matthew Deer and Audrey Welch as they began their performance.

Matthew Deer pulled a drum from a bag at his side. He explained what the drum meant to his people, and he told how its round shape stands for the circle of life and balance. "The beating of the drum represents the heartbeat of Mother Earth," he explained. "This is why you are sitting in a circle—so that everyone is equal and important, like the balance of life."

Matthew Deer started to sing along with Audrey Welch to the beat of the drum. Some of the students laughed quietly, not knowing how to react to this new experience, but Tom sat quietly and listened.

After the drum song, both performers took turns telling the stories of their people—Tom's people. They told stories about how their people came to be and stories that taught lessons, in which animals acted like humans. The nervous laughter stopped. Now, the laughter was in response to the funny parts in some of the stories.

Tom sat without moving, soaking up all he heard. He felt overwhelmed. Tom wondered if his father had told him any of these stories as a young child. Before he knew it, the performance was over. Tom waited as Matthew Deer and Audrey Welch answered the students' questions. Then Matthew Deer came up to Tom.

"So you're Lance's son. You were only about this high the last time I saw you," Matthew said, putting his hand at waist level.

"You remember me?" Tom asked, surprised.

"Sure I do. Your mother used to cook us some great meals," Matthew said. Tom couldn't believe it—there was so much he wanted to ask about his dad and about his heritage. Suddenly, the second period bell rang. He had been so excited that he forgot about his next class.

"You'd better get going," Matthew Deer said, grabbing a piece of paper and pen from his bag and writing something down.

"I'd love to talk with you some more," he said. "We are going to a Native American social gathering at this address tonight at 7:30. It would be great if you could make it."

Matthew Deer handed Tom the paper. Tom looked at the address. It was within walking distance of his apartment.

"Sorry I don't have a phone number to give you," Matthew said. "The friends I'm staying with just moved here and their phone isn't hooked up yet. Audrey and I will be heading back home early tomorrow morning."

"I'll be sure to make it. Your friends live only about five blocks from my apartment," Tom said as he started toward the door.

"Great. I'll see you tonight," Matthew Deer said.

Tom was so excited that he could hardly pay attention in his classes. He thought about all the questions he could ask Matthew Deer. It wasn't until he saw Cassandra at lunchtime that he remembered what else he had planned for that night.

"How could I have forgotten the dance? How could I have forgotten Cassandra?" Tom said to himself.

Not only were the Native American gathering and dance both that night, but they were scheduled at the same time. There was no way he could go to both. Tom pulled the address Matthew Deer had given him out of his pocket and looked at it. As Matthew Deer had said, there was no phone number, no way to get in touch with him.

Tom thought about how important it was for him to talk with Matthew Deer. He also remembered how long he had wanted to have a date with Cassandra. If he broke their date at the last minute, she might be angry and never go out with him again. As he approached Cassandra, Tom decided what he would do. Sitting down at her table, he said, "Cassandra . . .

||||■ THINKING ABOUT THE STORY

1. Describe Tom's life.

2. What has Tom always wanted to know about?

3. Why is Tom anxious in the beginning of the story?

4. What does Tom learn at the Native American performance?

5. What decision must Tom make?

||||■ THINKING ABOUT THE ENDING

Tom Yellow Eagle is faced with a difficult decision. He must choose between learning more about his Native American heritage and keeping a special date. What thoughts and fears are in his mind as he makes his decision? What do you think he will decide to do?

Look back at what you have learned about Tom and the importance of the decision he faces. Write an ending to this story in which he either goes to the dance with Cassandra or to the Native American gathering.

The Luckiest Girl

by Cynthia Benjamin

September 6

I still can't believe what happened to me today. It seems like a dream. I was eating my lunch when David Allen sat down next to me. He said he saw me try out for the basketball team yesterday. He thinks I really aced the tryouts. If the coach doesn't pick me, David's going to punch him out. We must have talked for 20 minutes. After lunch, we walked to English class together. Everyone saw us. Joyce and Debbie said all the senior girls wanted to know who I was. When they found out I was just a sophomore, they wanted to die.

There I was, Anita Wade, walking with the best looking guy in school. I mean, David is everything. He's smart and popular, besides being incredibly cute. He was dating Rosie McDonald for almost a year. I can't figure out why Rosie split up with him. But she transferred to another school, so I don't have to worry about her.

I don't know how to describe it, but when David and I talked together, he made me feel really special. It was as if I were the only person in the world.

But that's not all. He was in the parking lot after school when I was leaving. At first, I thought it was a coincidence. But now I'm sure he stayed just to meet me. He drove me home. The last thing he did was to ask for my phone number. If he doesn't call me, I don't know what I'll do.

David called. Dad said he sounded very "polite" and "mature" on the phone. Dad wants to meet him when we go out on Friday. David said there's a terrific movie playing at the mall. He wanted to ask me sooner, but he thought I was still seeing Frank. I said we broke up. What I didn't say was that we broke up at the end of last year. I haven't dated anyone all summer. It was pretty weird not having anything to do. I felt really out of things. I don't anymore. When I called Joyce to tell her about David, she said I'm the luckiest girl in the class. You know something? I think she's right.

I have to write this all down before I go to bed. I just got back from my first date with David, and it was perfect. I don't think I've ever felt so happy in my entire life. After the movie, he took me to the cafe where the kids in the senior class hang out. Everyone stared when we walked in the door. It was like something out of a movie. David was real cool about it. He's probably used to everyone watching him. But I wasn't sure how to handle it. Even after we sat down, a few of the girls were looking at me. I know they were jealous because I was out with the most amazing guy in their class.

Then one of David's friends, Jamal, came over to our table. He said I was the coolest looking girl in the place. I felt terrific. But when I looked at David, I could see he was kind of upset. He told Jamal to back off. I thought he was joking, but now I'm not so sure. Anyway, Jamal left our table right away. David told me he doesn't like it when other guys come on to his girlfriend.

I went to a party with David this weekend. Everything has been going really well for us. I mean we see each other every day in school. Then David drives me home and calls me before I go to bed. But at the party, something kind of weird happened. David was talking to some of his friends, so I started talking to Jamal. All of a sudden, David grabbed my arm and yanked it. I told him to let go, but he wouldn't. He just held on to me harder. He said he didn't want me talking to any other guys. Then he started yelling at me because of the way I looked. He said you could see through my blouse.

"That's the only reason Jamal wants to talk to you," he said.

I was so shocked that I didn't know what to say. There was nothing wrong with the way I looked tonight. I knew my blouse was OK. But he kept going on and on. He said I was wearing too much makeup and to take it off in the bathroom. I couldn't believe he would say that to me, especially in front of his friends. I ran out of the house and down the street. Then I heard David calling my name. He ran after me and begged me to stop. When I turned around, he was crying. I mean really crying. I didn't know what to do. David said he gets jealous of me sometimes because he loves me so much. He's afraid someone will take me away from him. He thinks I'm beautiful. No one ever said that to me before.

_____
October 4

David and I went on a picnic today in Fairview Park. It was incredible. David brought me a bouquet of roses. When I opened the picnic basket, there was a small box inside. My hands were shaking so hard I could hardly unwrap it. It was a ring . . . a beautiful gold ring. David said that one day he'll buy me a diamond ring. For our honeymoon, he promised to take me on a round-the-world cruise.

_____
October 8

What did I do to make David get so mad at me? He

knows I have basketball practice on Tuesday afternoon. I didn't get out until almost 5:00. When I left school, David was waiting for me outside. I thought he was going to explode. I've never seen him so mad. He pulled me into his car. Then he said I was spending too much time hanging out with Joyce and Debbie. He said they would introduce me to other guys to break us up. That's crazy! Everyone knows how much I love David. But he wouldn't believe me. He wants me to stop talking to Joyce and Debbie and to quit the basketball team. I told him I wouldn't. There's no way I'm turning my back on my two best friends. That's when David hit me. For a minute, I couldn't say anything. No boy has ever hit me. I jumped out of his car and ran as fast as I could. He's called me four times tonight, but I won't talk to him.

Mom wants to know what's the matter. She and Dad really like David. If I tell her what happened, they won't let me see him. If I don't date David, who will I go out with? All the other good guys have girlfriends already. I can't go back to staying at home all the time. I just can't.

I don't know what to do.

October 11
_____

David and I made up. I made him promise he would never hit me again. He said he doesn't know why he did it. But there's this anger inside him sometimes. When something or someone really ticks him off, he loses control. He was worried because I've been spending time at basketball practice. He thinks it means I'm tired of him. I still don't understand how he could feel that way. I told him so, too. When he looked at me, his eyes were filled with tears. That's when he told me.

David said his mom had walked out on his dad when he was 6 years old. David has never forgiven her for that. He knows his dad was rough with her sometimes, but that doesn't excuse what she did. David really loves me. He loves me more than anyone in the world. He says that if I ever leave him, he's going to kill himself.

Things are OK between David and me. We've been seeing each other every afternoon. Today, he gave me an ankle bracelet with tiny diamonds in the silver chain. I know it must have cost a fortune. I asked him where he got the money.

"It's from my savings," he said. "I've been putting money away for college. But I'll spend it all on you if I have to."

I told him he didn't have to do things like that. It isn't right for him to spend his savings on presents for me. But he doesn't seem to care.

I told him I was quitting the basketball team. I know it's what he wants.

David beat me up yesterday. He saw me talking to Michael Greer. He's this really nice guy in my English class. Michael and I were just talking about the big test next week, that's all. But David gets so jealous sometimes. He was sitting in his car watching Michael and me. When Michael left, David followed me home. I was in front of the empty stores on Green Street when he grabbed me from behind. At first, I didn't know who it was, so I started to scream. That's when David punched me. He only stopped when a truck driver started yelling at him. David was so startled that he dropped my arm. I just took off. I didn't stop running until I got home. Mom and Dad were at work, so I double-locked the door.

I told Mom and Dad that I fell while I was roller blading. I couldn't bear to tell them the truth. If they knew what David did, they'd probably call the police or something. Whatever happened, they'd never let me see him again. I keep thinking about what David told me. "If I lose you, I'll kill myself, Anita. I really will."

He means it. I couldn't live with myself if anything happened to David.

November 4

I've talked to Joyce about what happened between David and me. She promised she wouldn't tell anyone what he did. Besides, Joyce told me other guys in our school hit their girlfriends. No one thinks it's a big deal or anything, and none of the girls have turned in their boyfriends. If I did say anything about what David did, I'm afraid the other kids would find out.

I really don't know what to do. I feel so confused. A part of me is still worried that David might hurt himself. But I'm scared of him, too. David has called me every night, but I won't talk to him. When I see him waiting for me outside of school, I hide. Until I figure out what to do, I'm going to stay away from David.

November 6

David's been following me home from school in his car. Then he sits outside my house until my parents get home from work. A few nights, I've seen him in our backyard late at night. He just stares up at my window, as if he's waiting for me to come down.

Tonight, he called the house again. My parents weren't home, and I thought Dad might be calling me from the store. That's the only reason I answered the phone. But it was David. He pleaded with me not to hang up. He started to apologize for hitting me. That's when I told him to leave me alone. I've never said that to David before. But that's the way I feel right now. I need time away from him.

David sent me a bouquet of roses today. They arrived just before dinner. There was a card. It said, "Please give me one more chance. I love you very much. David." When I read it, I started to cry. Mom wanted to know if anything's wrong between David and me. She knows we haven't been seeing each other. What she doesn't know is why. Before I could answer her, the telephone rang.

When I picked up the receiver, my heart was pounding. I knew it would be David, and I was right. He wanted to know if I had received the flowers. He told me again how much he loved me. Then he asked me what I was going to do. I looked over at my mother. She could tell by my voice that something was wrong. I knew she would be able to help me. But she couldn't do anything unless I explained what had been going on. Then I heard David's voice. He kept saying, "Give me another chance. Please, Anita, I need you." My throat was dry. I swallowed hard, then I said . . .

IIIIITHINKING ABOUT THE STORY

1. When David and Anita first meet, does he say anything that shows he has a temper and could be violent? Explain.

2. Write three adjectives that describe Anita and three that describe David.

3. Why do you think David wants Anita to quit the basketball team and stop seeing her friends? What does this show about him?

4. Why do you think Anita is first attracted to David?

5. Why do you think she stays with him even after he abuses her?

6. Do you think Anita is "the luckiest girl"? Explain.

IIII■THINKING ABOUT THE ENDING

Think about what you have learned about Anita and David's relationship. Consider how David treats her and how she responds to his actions. Now Anita has to make an important decision, one that will affect the future of her relationship with David.

Write an ending for Anita's last journal entry that describes what she did when David called her. This ending should be based on how Anita thinks and feels in this situation. Remember to write it in the first person.

Darnell's Dilemma

by Wiley M. Woodard

Darnell was never happier to see 8:00 P.M. come. It had been a long day at school and a grueling evening at his part-time job in a fast-food restaurant. Finally, it was quitting time. "If I had to smile and ask another customer if I could help them, I don't know what I'd do," Darnell thought.

"Goodnight, Mr. O'Reilly," he said to his crew chief as he headed towards the employee lounge. He removed his smock, balled it up, and shoved it in his locker. "I wish I didn't have to give up the drama club for this," he muttered to himself. Darnell worked so he could help out at home. His father's dreams of small-business success had been crushed by the recession. Instead of running a construction business, he still worked for one. His mother worked a part-time job that didn't bring in much money and took a few classes at the local college.

His parents had to run the house, pay bills, and take care of his little brother and sister. Darnell didn't want to be an added burden. He got a job so he could at least buy his own school clothes.

As he headed out the back door of the restaurant, Darnell saw his friend Brad still at work on the counter. Brad was a senior and a basketball star. Darnell admired him because he excelled both on the basketball court and in class. Like Darnell, Brad worked so he could help his parents with household expenses.

"On your way out, little man?" Brad asked.

"You know it," Darnell replied with a grin.

"I'll check you out later, man," Brad said as Darnell

bounded out the door. The crisp autumn air made him shiver a bit, even though he was wearing a light jacket.

"Hi, Darnell," Coni said sweetly, walking towards him with a group of her friends.

"What's up, Coni?" Darnell replied.

"I'm just on my way to Cheryl's house. Want to hang out with us for a while?" Coni asked.

"No, thanks. I got some things to do," Darnell said. He was on his way home to do homework, but he was afraid Coni might think that wasn't very cool. "I would love to go out with her," he thought, turning around to watch Coni as she continued on her way to Cheryl's with her friends. Sighing, he headed home.

Darnell was proud to help his parents make ends meet, but he knew that if they saw his grades slip even a little, they'd make him quit his job. Not a day went by that his father didn't remind him about the importance of a good education. By now, Darnell could recite his father's speeches word for word. He could hear him exclaim, "Our ancestors fought so our people could have a decent education. I won't see their efforts wasted. It's too important to your future."

Darnell could hear the sounds of slow jams playing on the radio, children laughing, and an occasional siren blare, sounds that reminded him he was almost home. He began to walk to the beat of his favorite song, silently singing to himself, and barely noticing the storefront churches and grocery stores he passed along the way. This neighborhood was the only place Darnell and his family had ever called home, but he dreamed of the day they could afford to move elsewhere. He wanted a big backyard, so that his father could have the garden he was always talking about, his mother could dry their clothes in the fresh air, and his little brother and sister could have plenty of space to play.

"What's up, Darnell?" a voice called from nearby.

Darnell turned around to see his friend, Speed. "Hey, what's up?" he asked.

Speed had been just one grade ahead of Darnell before he dropped out of school. It was too bad because he had been an excellent student. He had the smarts, talent, and ability to become anything he wanted. Instead, Speed chose to sell drugs.

"Done flipping burgers for the day?" he asked.

"Yeah," replied a weary Darnell.

"I keep telling you, man, you're working harder than you have to," said Speed.

"I'm making honest money," Darnell replied.

"You're making honest chump change," teased Speed. "I bet you had to save two years of paychecks to afford those sneakers. I could make the same money in less than a half-hour."

"I'm not complaining," replied Darnell.

"Look at you, you're so tired you can barely stand up," Speed continued. "A brother shouldn't have to work that hard. Our ancestors worked hard enough."

"Speaking of ancestors, do you think yours would be proud of how you're making your money?" Darnell asked.

"I saw my grandfather and my father work themselves to death," Speed snapped back. "I'm not going out like that."

"Keep doing what you're doing, and you may be going out sooner than you think," Darnell warned.

"You watch too much TV, man," said Speed. "Maybe that's where you got the bright idea that working hard in a fast-food joint will take you away from here. Face it, man. You're never going to be President of the United States, and neither will your kids."

"Come on, Speed," said Darnell. "That kind of thinking will never get you anywhere."

"Neither will making shakes and fries. There's a big world out here, man, and it's just waiting for you to conquer it!" exclaimed Speed.

"I'll conquer it my way. You conquer it yours," Darnell replied.

"My way could be your way," said Speed. "Just come out for a few months—you could help your parents wipe out most of their bills. Look at Raj. Six months ago, he was thinking just like you. Now, you couldn't pay him to give up the good life!"

"That's what I'm afraid of," said Darnell.

"There's nothing to be afraid of out here, baby. I got your back," said Speed with a smile. "I won't let anything happen to you."

Darnell surprised himself by taking Speed seriously. He pondered his offer for a moment.

"Can you look me in the eyes and honestly tell me your family couldn't use the extra boost?" Speed asked.

"No," Darnell replied softly.

"All right then. I tell you, a man with your smarts can make a killing out here. You can make more than enough money for college in no time," Speed said.

"Speed," Darnell said, "I think—"

"Don't think; just act. What's it gonna be, little man?" Speed demanded.

Darnell took a deep breath and said . . .

IIII THINKING ABOUT THE STORY

1. List three adjectives that describe Darnell.

2. What does Darnell think of Speed?

3. Why do Darnell's parents want him to stay in school?

4. Do you think that Darnell's parents would accept his giving in to Speed's offer to sell drugs, even if it was for just a little while? Why or why not?

5. Why does Darnell suddenly take Speed seriously?

IIII THINKING ABOUT THE ENDING

Think about what you learned about Darnell and Speed. Do you think that Darnell will give in to Speed and sell drugs? Why or why not? Write an ending for the story in which you use what you learned about Darnell's dreams and frustrations to predict the choice he will make.

Apple

by Krista Kanenwisher

Jim Big Bear, a Native American from the Crow Nation of Montana, had worried about going back to high school. He had never felt a part of the school community before he dropped out, and going back to class was difficult.

But last fall, a friend had talked Jim into seeing a counselor. Somehow, Jim found himself in school. Getting into the classwork had been hard, and he was assigned to Apple, a tutor who would help him make up a semester of classes.

Jim tried not to let Apple know he liked her at all. She would come and drag him out of bed on the mornings he didn't show up for class.

At first, he had resisted, but then he found that he enjoyed checking into the Native American Education office and teasing the counselors and tutors. Perhaps he and Apple had survived as a tutor–student team because she had discovered how to push his "guilt button."

Even Jim's mom enjoyed Apple's friendship. Having moved Jim and herself out of Crow Agency and off the reservation, she had not made a real friend until Apple came along. Jim had begun to sense a peacefulness in his life—until last night.

The memory of his mom rose in Jim's chest once again. She was hit by a car while crossing the street in the rain. Jim and his mom had been on their own all his life. Now he was the only one left. Jim wondered why he should care about high school, eating, or even getting up. Pushing his head under the pillow, Jim tried to make his mind a complete blank.

Apple came into Jim's room, picked up his clothes, and fumbled for something to do or say. "Jim, there are some things that we need to do this morning. We need to call the rest of your family and tell them what's happened to your mother. We need to call the school and let them know you won't be in today."

"Look, there's no one to call, and you can tell the school I won't be in. Ever," replied Jim.

The next few days were a blur. Apple was there for the funeral and burial of his mother. She was there first thing every morning trying to persuade Jim to look at his books or go back to school. Then, one day, Apple did not come. Jim fumbled through the day trying to make sense out of his life. Several times, he walked around the kitchen staring at his homework and the books she had left neatly piled at one end of the table.

After missing a week of school, Jim wondered about the kids in his classes, and he even thought about the teachers. Who would have believed he'd miss old man Trumble's class? Jim was at least a year older than most of the students, and he felt apart from them. But he liked Trumble and history, and he even liked reading. Apple had given him several books to read during one of their early tutorials— *Winter in the Blood* by James Welch, a Blackfoot from Browning. How did it start? "Going home was never easy. . . ."

You got that right, thought Jim. Tossing the book into his bag, he had never intended to read it. But without a television, he had spent some evening hours looking for something to do and picked up the novel. He spent that winter reading one book after another. He liked reading novels about people like himself.

Looking around the room, he saw a bookshelf filled with used paperbacks and old history books. His mom had dragged the bookshelf home one day. At first Jim had intended to slap a coat of paint on it and get the books off the floor as quickly as possible. Instead, he started to draw native designs on the old stained wood. He and his mom spent the winter painting the intricate patterns.

He lifted the shades for the first time in a long while. He was surprised to find the day sunny. The sunlight in the room began to warm Jim, and he suddenly felt in a hurry to go out. He found himself headed west down 21st Street. Because he didn't have anyplace else to go, he wound up in front of Great Falls High. Classes were already over for the day. What was he doing here?

Suddenly feeling awkward, Jim turned back. He began to relax as he strolled home, relieved that he wouldn't run into anyone that late in the afternoon. Walking east on 21st Street, he was unaware that he was being followed by a carload of giggling teenage girls.

The car nearly hit him as it rolled over the curb and came to an abrupt stop. The girls hopped out and started asking questions all at once. Where had he been? What was he doing? When was he coming back to school? He didn't have to worry about responding to their questions because they didn't seem to be waiting for the answers. "Good thing," he thought, "because I don't have any answers." As quickly as they had come, they were back in the car and off down the road.

Jim hated returning to his apartment. It had been fun seeing the girls from the Native American Club. They were the first friends he had made in his 12 years of schooling. So much had changed that year.

Back home again, Jim sat down to open his algebra book. Could he catch up? He tried to figure out some problems. After an hour, he checked his answers. Jim was not surprised to find that more than half of his answers were wrong. Disappointed, he put down the algebra book and looked for something to eat.

Then all the old discouraging voices came back. Hopelessness moved in on him like an old, familiar friend. In a strange way, his giving up seemed comforting. At least, he knew what giving up felt like. It was succeeding that frightened him. He was afraid because success meant taking a giant leap into the dark and trying over and over again. How long would it take to try again? How long would it take before he was not alone, or unhappy, or struggling through high school?

Turning on the radio, Jim thought about math. "Why is it," he thought, "that if you are smart in English or history, or if you are exceptional in art, no one thinks anything of it. But if you are a good student in math, you are brilliant."

Jim grabbed his jacket and went out. He headed south toward the bowling alley. He didn't want to run into those girls again. He skirted the block with the fast-food places where the kids might be and made it to the bowling alley without being seen.

Inside it was dark. A guy about his age was draped over the pool table shooting while his friend watched. Jim thought he'd watch for awhile, but the second man was loud and got on his nerves. He moved around the alley to the cashier, paid for a game, and rented some shoes. After his first few balls, Jim realized that his game was off. He played out the game and went home.

The early spring air had turned chilly, and Jim zipped up his jacket. There was a crispness in the air that reminded him of Crow Agency, Montana, and of his grandparents' home on the reservation. He liked being with them. He could almost smell the fry bread and the wood-burning stove. Grandmother still wore the traditional leggings and wide leather belt on her house dress. Both she and Grandfather had long braids and toothy smiles. The Montana winds had creased their faces, making great crevices.

Jim did not turn on a light when he entered his apartment and settled into a chair. He tried to picture Grandfather. Like the other elders of the Crow Nation, Grandfather Big Bear in his senior years was still tall and sturdy. Jim floated into a quiet sleep.

Toward morning, he awoke. He had been in the chair for hours. He took off his jacket and headed to the kitchen to make himself a pot of coffee.

Coffee, toast, and a little bacon were as close to fry bread and Indian corn as he would get at 5:00 A.M. In the premorning glow, Jim noticed a note taped to the kitchen cupboard. It was a note he and his mom had made: "Goals: I, Verna, will take a vocational class. I, Jim, will finish high school." They had ceremoniously signed the document.

After showering and cleaning up, Jim sat back down at the table. He began to redo the math problems, and finally, waiting as long as he could, he picked up the phone. Jim felt a mixture of hope and despair.

"Hello?" said Apple at the other end.

Jim hesitated. Would he continue with school or tell her he was quitting? He made his decision, took a deep breath, and said . . .

1. Why was Jim Big Bear alone?

2. Do you think Jim likes high school?

3. Jim has dropped out of high school once before. Do you think this time is different from the first time he dropped out? How?

4. How has Apple made a difference in Jim's life?

5. At the end of the story, Jim calls Apple. Why do you think he has called her?

6. Jim has an important decision to make. What is it?

||||■ THINKING ABOUT THE ENDING

Jim Big Bear has a great deal to think about. He might return to high school, drop out, go home to live with his grandparents, or a number of other options.

Use what you have learned about Jim to write an ending to this story. Make sure you tell why Jim made his decision and what effect it will have on his life.

Surviving Your Parents' Divorce

by Cynthia Benjamin

When Juan woke up in his bedroom on Sunday morning, he felt confused. He looked around. There were his basketball trophies on top of his bookcase. His math book was still open on his desk, just where it had been since Thursday. Everything in his bedroom looked familiar. But somehow it felt different. Juan sighed. "That's the way it's been since the divorce," he thought. "I'd better get used to it."

For the past six months, Juan had been living part of the time with his mother and part of the time with his father. Because his parents lived in the same neighborhood, this wasn't as bad as it sounded. He was able to attend the same high school and keep the same friends.

As Juan dressed, he wondered what his father would be doing this weekend. That was part of the problem with this joint custody arrangement. Juan always missed the parent he wasn't staying with. "Oh well," he thought, "maybe that will get easier as time goes on. After all, Dad said I could call him anytime this weekend." But there was something else bothering Juan. He wasn't sure if the problem would go away, either. After he finished making his bed, he sat there with his head in his hands. He knew he had to talk to someone about it. But he wasn't sure who would understand how he felt. Then he heard his mother calling him for breakfast.

Juan and his mother spent almost the entire day sanding and painting her living-room bookcases. At the end of the afternoon, they were both proud of their work. "We make a pretty good team," his mother said. "Come on, now it's time for the fun part. I'm going to need your help unpacking those boxes. You wouldn't believe how many books and files I keep at home for my classes."

Juan groaned and held up his hand. "No way, Mom. My bad back just kicked in." But he was laughing, too. A part of him was proud of being able to help his mother, just as a part of him was proud of her for going back to school. They liked to joke about both of them having to study for finals.

By dinnertime, they were both exhausted. Instead of cooking, Juan's mother ordered a pizza. They ate it in the kitchen. From time to time, Mrs. Perez looked at her watch. Juan knew what she was thinking. It was almost time for him to leave her house and bicycle back to his father's. Juan called it "changing houses." Whenever he did it, he got a funny feeling in his stomach. He loved both of his parents. If only they could have worked out their problems. If only. . . "Well, it's no use thinking about that now," Juan thought.

He looked over at his mother as he finished the last bite of his pizza. "Time for me to go, Mom," he said. He saw his mother frown slightly and bite her lip. Juan knew she felt as sad as he did. His mother had once described the feeling as "shifting emotional gears." Juan understood what she meant. "At least, I don't have a suitcase," he said to his mother as he helped her clean up the kitchen table.

"Not even a toothbrush in your jacket pocket," his mother added. They were standing at the kitchen door. Juan's school books were in his bookbag.

His mother tried to smile as she kissed him goodbye. "Do me a favor. Be careful crossing Second Avenue on your bike," she said.

Juan sighed. "Mom, I'm 15 years old, and I've been riding a bike in this neighborhood since I was three."

"I know," his mother said. "Remember: I'm the one who taught you how to ride."

Juan was getting his bike from the garage when his mother called from the open kitchen door. "Remind your father to call your dentist. You're due for your checkup this month."

"Will do," Juan answered. He walked his bike across the backyard.

"Honey, there's one more thing," his mother called.

Juan gripped the bike handles more tightly. He knew what his mother was going to say even before she said it.

"Please tell your father that I'm waiting for the check," she said.

"OK," Juan called back as he left the backyard. He thought about his mother's words as he rode back to his dad's house. He really didn't know too much about the financial details of his parents' divorce. But he could almost imagine the look on his father's face when he relayed his mother's message. He knew his dad wouldn't lose his temper. Instead, he would talk to Juan about the problems he'd been having at the store recently. When he was finished, he'd say, "When you see your mother on Thursday, let her know I'm doing the best I can. Tell her to be patient. I'll send the check soon."

Juan pedaled so fast that the October wind cut against his cheeks. The sharpness of the air surprised him at first. But it also gave him more energy. It felt good just to ride down Green Street past the park. For the first time in weeks, he wasn't thinking about what he would say to one parent or the other. Boy, that was a relief.

Juan reached his father's house at 6:30. He saw his dad watching the street from the living-room window. When Juan pulled his bike into the driveway, his father came out to meet him.

"It's good to have you back," he said as they walked into the house together. "How was your weekend?"

Juan told his father about the basketball game he and his mother went to on Friday night. His father loved basketball almost as much as he did, and they practiced together whenever they could. But this time his father didn't sound very enthusiastic.

"Since when has your mother been interested in basketball?" was all he said at first.

Juan just shrugged. "She told me she's trying to learn the game."

His father didn't smile. "I bet that guy she started dating is into it. I think he's a coach for some college team." Then he turned to face Juan. "Have you met him yet?" he asked.

Juan shook his head and headed for his room. "I really don't know anything about him, Dad," he said as he climbed the stairs. When he reached his bedroom, Juan shut the door and started to unpack his bookbag, but he didn't feel like studying for his English exam. "Things were a lot easier before the divorce," he thought before going to bed.

The next day, when Juan came home from basketball practice, his father was making dinner. He lifted the lid from the pot and smiled proudly at Juan.

"I borrowed your grandmother's stew recipe. What do you think?" he asked.

"It smells great, Dad," Juan said. His father had come a long way as a cook. Juan looked more closely at the contents of the pot. "So far you haven't burnt the sauce. That's a real first. I'm proud of you." While Juan prepared the salad, he talked to his father about basketball practice.

"Man, I can't believe how nice it is just to have dinner with Dad," Juan thought. "It's the first time I haven't been worried that he's going to ask me something about Mom."

The phone rang. Juan's father answered it. When he came back into the kitchen, his voice sounded tight. "It's your mother," he said. "She wants to talk to you about something."

As Juan walked into the living room, he got a funny feeling in the pit of his stomach. He knew his mother would ask what his father had said about sending the check. There was only one problem—so far, Juan hadn't mentioned it to him. He picked up the telephone receiver. "Why do my parents always do this to me?" he thought.

But he was pleasantly surprised. His mother was calling to remind him about his birthday in another two weeks. As if Juan could forget!

"I have a special surprise for you," she said. "Your grandmother's coming down for a few days especially to see you. So I decided to take you both to that new restaurant on Claremont Avenue. After that, it's your choice, as long as it's not basketball. Your grandmother hates it."

Juan smiled. He could remember all the times his grandmother had told him what a waste of time basketball was. But because it was Juan's favorite sport, she had learned all she could about it. He was really looking forward to seeing her.

Juan's excitement faded when he told his father about his plans. "Of course you should see your grandmother," his dad said. "But I thought we were going to celebrate your birthday together. In fact, I already ordered two tickets to a basketball game as a surprise." Juan swallowed hard and looked down at his plate. He knew what was coming next.

"It's up to you, son," his father said. "After all, it's your birthday. You should do what you want to do."

"Terrific," Juan thought. "I'm being asked to choose between Mom and Dad, and on my birthday no less." He spent the rest of the meal moving the food around on his plate. He didn't feel very hungry at all.

After dinner, he went to shoot some baskets in the park with his friend Tony. The practice was a disaster. Each time, Juan's basketball tap-danced its way around the rim of the basket before falling to the ground.

"Hey, what's wrong with you tonight, my friend?" Tony asked. "This is basketball, remember? Like we've only been playing together since we were 9 years old, right?"

Juan tried one more shot before giving up in disgust. "Sorry, man. I guess it's my concentration. I've got other things on my mind."

"That I can see," Tony said. "Why don't you tell me about it? I know it will be less depressing than watching you try to shoot baskets."

"It's my parents," Juan began.

Tony whistled and threw his basketball high in the air. "So what isn't? I remember what it was like after my mom and dad broke up. Definitely not the greatest time, right?"

Juan nodded. He wasn't sure where to begin, so he just blurted it out. "They make me feel like the wishbone at a turkey dinner. I'm always being torn in half."

Tony slapped him on the back and smiled. "I know the feeling well," he said. "My parents did exactly the same thing. They were always asking me to pass messages from one to the other."

For the first time, Juan felt a little better. So he wasn't the only person in the world it had happened to. "You're right," he said to Tony. "Sometimes, I feel more like a delivery boy than their son. Now I'm being asked to choose who I'll spend my birthday with this year. I'd just as soon pass on the whole thing."

The two boys stopped in front of Juan's house. "Look," Tony said. "There's only one way to deal with it. You have to be up front about your feelings. If your parents are making it tough for you, tell them. They can't fix it if they don't even know it's broken."

Juan zipped up his jacket. Was it getting cold or was he just scared about talking to his mother and father? He honestly didn't know. He slapped Tony on the back. "Thanks, man," he said. "See you in school tomorrow."

When Juan hung up his jacket in the hall closet, he could hear his father getting a snack in the kitchen. He remembered Tony's words. Who would he spend his birthday with? Was there a way to make both parents happy? Juan looked at his father, sitting at the kitchen table. He turned to him and said . . .

IIII■ THINKING ABOUT THE STORY

1. How has Juan's life changed in the past year?
2. How does he feel about the joint-custody arrangement?
3. What special problems must Juan deal with since his parents' divorce?
4. Why does talking to his friend Tony help Juan?
5. What does Tony mean by "they can't fix it if they don't know it's broken"?
6. How does Juan feel about his birthday? Why does he feel this way?

||||■THINKING ABOUT THE ENDING

Juan feels as if he's being torn between his parents. Think about what you've learned about Juan and his parents. How has his relationship with his parents changed since the divorce? Do you think it is important for Juan to tell his parents about his feelings? Why or why not?

Review what you've concluded about Juan and his relationship with his parents to predict what he'll do. Then write an ending for the story that clearly shows the decision he makes.

The Phantom Car

by Gerald Tomlinson

David slowly walked north on Garfield Street.
His watch read a few minutes before 3:00. It was a Monday
afternoon. David carried a paper bag that held a quart of
chocolate-swirl ice cream. His older sister had given him the
money for it that morning before school.

As he neared First Savings Bank, he saw a car double-
parked just beyond the bank's entrance. Garfield Street was
a busy, four-lane street, and to see a double-parked car on it
was not unusual. But there was something about this dark-
gray sedan that caught David's eye.

It was the car's odd-looking driver. Bright sunlight
reflected off the windshield and made it hard to see his
features clearly. Still, David was quite sure that the man
behind the wheel was former President Ronald Reagan.
Impossible! David looked closer at the man. He realized that
the man was wearing a rubber Halloween mask of the former President.

Just then, three masked men in business suits burst
through the front door of the bank. David recognized them
all. The man in the lead, carrying a black satchel, was ex-
President Richard Nixon. Right at his heels, toting a brown
paper shopping bag, came a tall, thin man with a slight
limp—Frankenstein's monster. Bringing up the rear was a
short, stocky circus clown with reddish hair.

David realized that he had walked into the middle of a
bank robbery. No sooner had the clown tumbled into the
back seat of the gray sedan than David heard the wail of
police sirens in the distance.

71

He watched as the getaway car roared north on Garfield. Curiously, only a few people seemed to pay much attention to it. Within a few seconds, the gray sedan cut to the right, skidding around the corner onto Fourth Avenue.

David raced toward the bank. A uniformed guard staggered out the door, gun drawn. He was yelling, "Holdup!" but by then the gray sedan had disappeared.

Running at full speed, David came to Fourth Avenue His quick glance took in the whole length of the street, all the way down the sloping hill to the Converse River. The getaway car was gone. The street, busy as ever, showed no sign that anything was wrong. A couple of well-dressed pedestrians strolled along, looking perfectly calm.

David turned and headed back toward the bank at a slower pace. He was an eyewitness, the *only* eyewitness to see the fleeing robbers. He knew what they looked like—or at least what their masks looked like. He could describe the car, right down to the make and model. He'd noticed a dent near the right taillight. He'd even memorized the first half of the license-plate: G73.

Sergeant Rinaldi, a slim detective with a mustache, soon arrived at the crime scene. He talked to David for what seemed like hours. David's chocolate-swirl gradually turned to mush. Rinaldi took careful notes of everything David said.

"Son," Sergeant Rinaldi said at last, "you've been a great help. We'll have these guys in no time."

He spoke too soon. Three days after the heist, David read a five-line item in the newspaper that said the trail was cold. Except for David, no one on Garfield Street or Fourth Avenue that Monday afternoon seemed to have observed the getaway car.

David couldn't believe it. The police had all sorts of clues. How many G73 license plates could there be in Arnold City? How could a gray sedan turn east on Fourth Avenue and just disappear into thin air?

David decided to tackle the case on his own. He was sure that the dark-gray car had stopped somewhere between Garfield and Hayes Streets. The robbers had piled out with the loot and made their escape. But where and how?

The next day after school, David went back to the bank. Traffic was heavier than on the day of the robbery. As he looked toward the corner, he remembered exactly what he had seen.

David continued walking north on Garfield Street to Fourth Avenue. This was the crucial location. The car could not have gone more than a block farther, or he would have seen it. At some point before reaching Hayes Street, it had vanished.

On his left, less than a third of the way down the street, stood a large parking garage. "Park" the sign said, and an arrow showed where. The gray sedan could have swung into the opening beside the arrow. But then what?

As David glanced into the garage, he saw a parking attendant in a white shirt and black slacks. He walked in.

"Excuse me," he said. "My name's David Snead. Were you on duty Monday when the bank was robbed?"

The attendant, a red-haired man, strongly built but shorter than David, growled, "What's it to you, kid?"

"I just wondered if you saw the gray car with the four robbers in it. All four of them were wearing masks."

"I see lots of gray cars. Now beat it. I got work to do." The attendant turned and walked toward the rear of the garage. David noticed that he was about the same height and weight as the bank-robbing clown.

Staring after him, David shouted, "They were wearing masks!"

Without turning, the attendant waved back at him in annoyance. "Yeah, and I'm Ronald Reagan," he yelled. "Get lost."

David returned to the street and stood for a moment, thinking. A red delivery van stood in front of a stationery store on Fourth Avenue. A wide metal ramp sloped down from the rear of the truck to the street. A woman wearing a baseball cap was wheeling a hand truck with two large cardboard boxes down the ramp.

David recalled the same place four days earlier. A much larger white van had been parked there then. He thought of the metal ramp. Could the getaway car have been driven up a similar ramp into the van and made its getaway? If so, someone *must* have noticed it.

David went into the stationery store, where the first clerk he saw was an elderly woman wearing pink-rimmed eyeglasses and a bright print dress.

"Hi," he said. "Could I ask you a question?"

"Go right ahead, young man," said the woman.

"Were you working here on the day of the bank robbery?" David asked.

She smiled. "The police get younger and younger, don't they? You're a rookie, I guess."

"I'm a student," David said. "I saw the robbery on the way home from school."

"Well, aren't you lucky? What's the question?"

"Did you see the gray car with the robbers go by here on the day the bank was held up?" he asked hopefully.

The woman shook her head. "Do you know how many cars drive by here on an average day, young man? Hundreds. Maybe thousands. I don't watch them. Nobody does."

"But this car was speeding," continued David. "It skidded around the corner from Garfield Street. I'm pretty sure there was a white van in front of your store when it happened."

"Oh, yes," the woman nodded. "A white van. That would be from the Barclay Company, delivering envelopes. I was stocking shelves in the back of the store when it arrived. Their driver is Phil Renfrew. You could ask him about what he saw. He should be coming by in about ten minutes."

David thanked her and left. He intended to come back,

but first he wanted to check out a business in a building at the end of the block.

Hank's Auto Repair occupied a one-story red brick building with a hand-painted sign over its three overhead doors. Some of the kids whispered that Hank's was a chop shop—a place where stolen cars were torn down and sold for parts. David had never believed this story. If the kids knew about it, so would the police. Besides, Hank's Auto Repair had been in business for as long as David could remember.

Hank himself was standing outside his garage when David approached. He knew the balding, gap-toothed owner by sight, but he had never spoken to him before.

"Hello," he said. "My name's David Snead. I wonder if you heard about the big bank robbery on Monday?"

"The Halloween heist?" Hank replied in a booming voice. "Sure. Four guys in a gray car. The cops think I was in on it. They think I cut the car apart. They even think I might have been wearing the Nixon mask." He chuckled. "Can you believe that? I'm an honest auto mechanic."

"You didn't see the gray getaway car?" David asked.

"I didn't see a thing. I was home in bed with the flu that day. None of my men saw anything either. They were busy working."

David was getting nowhere. He decided to go back to the stationery store and see if Phil Renfrew had shown up yet.

As he walked back toward Garfield Street, a tall, thin man stepped out of a doorway. David hesitated and almost turned back. He noticed that the man moved with a slight limp. With some alarm, he remembered that one of the bank robbers had moved with the same kind of limp. The man stopped directly in front of David.

"Hello, David," he said in a low, menacing voice. "You should just forget about what you saw last Monday. You're asking a lot of questions, and that could be dangerous. Very dangerous."

Before David could speak, the man was gone. Should he continue his investigation or stop and avoid the danger the man hinted at? David pondered the question and arrived at a decision. He would . . .

‖‖‖■THINKING ABOUT THE STORY

1. What does David see as he walks home from school?
2. Why does David decide to look into the case himself?
3. David is sure the car disappeared on Fourth Avenue between Garfield and Hayes Streets. Why is he so sure?
4. What are the three possible ways David thinks the gray sedan might have vanished?
5. Do you think any of the people David questions might be the bank robbers? Explain.

‖‖‖■THINKING ABOUT THE ENDING

David has not solved the case, but his questions have clearly worried someone. Using what David has learned about the bank robbery, write an ending for the story. Answer this question: Do you think David should drop the case? Why or why not? Think about what has happened so far. Consider the danger David may face if he keeps on asking questions.

Required for Graduation

by Kristen Shepos

Penny watched the last stragglers come down the front steps of the high school. Last period had ended at least 15 minutes ago, but Katarín was late as usual. Leaning on her backpack full of homework, Penny sighed. "There's no way around it," she thought. "Summer is definitely over." It wasn't that she didn't like school, but being a sophomore was so . . . well, in-between. She wasn't an interesting new face anymore, but she hadn't been around long enough to be noticeable, either.

"Even sophomore-year classes are boring," Penny thought. "No more easy stuff, but no electives, either." She took her schedule for the semester from the backpack and shook her head in disgust. Every subject was marked in the margin with a red "RFG"—Required For Graduation. She ran her finger down the list. Geometry, required. World history, required. English II, required. Computer literacy, required. Biology, required, *and* you had to dissect a frog. There was the Community Service requirement, too—one Saturday a month, she had to volunteer for whatever organization the school assigned her to. "Just what I need," Penny thought. "Now I have to give up my Saturdays, too." Things were not looking good for sophomore year.

"Hey, let's get out of here." Penny turned to find Katarín at the top of the steps with her hands on her hips.

"Are you ever on time?" she asked nastily. Reading the schedule had put her in a pretty foul mood.

"You really are in a bad mood. What's up? Did Eric Pelofsky try to kiss you in front of the class or something?"

Even Penny had to laugh at that. "It's just this dumb schedule, and this whole dumb high school thing," she complained. "I wish I were younger, or older, or something."

Katarín linked her arm through Penny's and said, "Would some junk food improve your mood? I have a Hamburger Heaven gift certificate that has to be used today or it expires. Think you can go for some fries and a chocolate shake?"

Things were looking up, Penny thought, as they walked down the sidewalk toward the restaurant.

"So what's your schedule like?" Penny asked.

"Pretty standard stuff," Katarín replied. "Geometry, History, English—nothing exciting."

"I know what you mean. Plus, now we have this stupid community service thing. . . ."

Katarín interrupted her before she could continue. "Stupid? You think that's a bad idea?"

"I just don't think it's fair that we have to give up one Saturday a month, and we don't even get to choose where we work." Penny's eyes narrowed in annoyance.

"Well, I think it's a great idea," Katarín said with a shrug. "I can't wait until next weekend."

"Why, what'd you get assigned to?"

"I'm a volunteer at the health clinic on Third Avenue, the one that specializes in helping moms with newborn babies," Katarín said excitedly.

"No wonder you like the idea!" Penny exclaimed. "You've got a great job doing something fun. I'm assigned to the homeless shelter downtown. Can you believe that?"

"What's the big deal?" Katarín asked. "I think that's a pretty cool job. You know you're helping people who can really use it."

"How can you tell?" Penny asked.

"They're homeless," Katarín replied. "They're living on the street. The shelter helps them because they don't have—"

Penny interrupted her in mid-sentence. "But how do you know they really need help? I mean, I think it's sad that people are homeless. If they're on the street because they lost their job or something, that's one thing. But how can you tell those people from the druggies? How do you know that someone won't use the money people give them to buy their next fix?"

Katarín looked at her, but didn't answer.

"Is that a mean thing to say?" Penny asked.

"Maybe I don't understand what you're saying," Katarín said, "because I know you pretty well, and I never thought you were insensitive."

"Are you kidding me?" Penny exclaimed. "I practically trip over the bums on 13th Street every morning. The same crazy homeless people have been begging there since I was 12. The two guys who sit outside the bowling alley and that woman with the braids who hangs out on the corner—I remember when they first showed up. They really looked like they were trying to get themselves together, so the whole neighborhood was giving them money. Now look at them—the woman is so strung out, she can barely talk. The guys get so drunk that they scare people. My mom won't let me near the bowling alley anymore because of them."

"But that means they need help even more," Katarín said. "People stopped giving them money, so they really need the shelter."

"So they can get everyone there hooked on drugs and booze? I think it stinks that people run out of money, but from what I've seen, it only happens if you're messed up enough to get yourself into trouble. Then it's your own fault." Penny shrugged. "What's wrong with not wanting to help people who mess themselves up?"

Katarín sighed in frustration. "Forget it. Right now, I just want some junk food." They pushed open the glass doors and stepped into the restaurant. Penny sniffed the air approvingly.

Picking up a tray piled high with fries and two large chocolate shakes, Katarín headed towards an open table near the window. "That way we can people-watch," she said. Penny could only nod, because her mouth was already full of fries. They settled down into the yellow plastic seats.

"So, are you going to volunteer at the shelter?" Katarín asked between long slurps of milkshake.

"I guess I have no choice," Penny answered, grabbing another handful of fries. "Anyway, there might be some people there who really deserve the help. But if I think someone's on drugs, I'm backing off. Another volunteer can deal with that person."

Katarín sighed and shook her head. "I really don't want to talk about this anymore. Let's talk about school."

"OK. What do you think of the new geometry teacher?" Penny said.

"Not bad. He tells funny stories. This morning, he stopped teaching and told us about the time he went to the dentist and . . ." Katarín continued with the story, but Penny wasn't listening. Something outside the window had caught her attention.

A man and a little girl were walking across the grass in front of Hamburger Heaven. The girl's chubby little hand grasped the man's left index finger. She was so small that her arm was too short to reach up and hold onto his entire hand.

Penny thought that the man looked about 30. He was dressed in filthy purple pants, and his squinty eyes peered out from beneath the hood of a faded winter coat. He carried an old backpack with a long bedroll balanced on the top. Lashed to the bedroll was the ripped bottom of an old cardboard box. Scrawled across it in black were the words
WE WILL WORK FOR FOOD.

The thought actually made Penny chuckle for a second. "What work could she possibly do?" Penny thought. "She can't be more than 3 years old!" Katarín stopped telling her story and looked at Penny.

"What's so funny?" she asked.

Penny was so focused on the pair that she didn't answer. She watched the man and the little girl walk up to a trash can outside the restaurant. As they got closer, she could see the neck of a bottle sticking out of the man's jacket pocket.

Katarín followed her gaze, and they watched the man remove the lid of the trash can and begin to dig through it. The little girl sat quietly on the grass.

Penny stared as the man replaced the lid of the can. Slowly, he shuffled towards another can right outside the window that she and Katarín were sitting by.

As he carefully sifted through the garbage, Penny looked closely at his face. Her first thought was that he bore no resemblance to the little girl—he had brown hair, brown eyes, and a dark complexion pitted with scars. Penny glanced at the fair-skinned child on the grass, then turned her attention back to the man, who was replacing the lid of the trash can. He quietly shuffled over to another one.

Katarín broke the silence. "That is so sad."

Penny said nothing for a moment. Then she replied, "I think he has a beer bottle in his pocket."

"What? How do you know?"

"I saw a bottle in his pocket."

Katarín's face flushed a deep red, and Penny knew she'd said the wrong thing. "You have no idea what that bottle is," Katarín said, her bottom lip trembling. "I can't believe how unfair you're being."

She's right, Penny thought. Here I am wiping fry grease off my fingers, and that guy is digging through other people's garbage. Even if it *was* a beer bottle, everyone had to eat, especially little kids. Penny felt a sudden surge of bravery and stood up. "Wait here," she told Katarín.

As she walked across the restaurant, Penny withdrew a five-dollar bill from the pocket of her shorts. Glancing at the menu, she saw that it would buy about three hamburgers and a couple of sodas. She took a deep breath and determinedly walked out the front door.

"Got any change, miss?" said the man.

Finished with his search of the trash, he had decided to stake out the front door. The little girl stood silently at his side, and for the first time Penny saw how small the child really was. She looked up, directly into the eyes of the man. He blinked quickly four or five times.

"Got any change?" he repeated.

Penny could see Katarín watching her through the window. Why are my hands shaking? she thought. Quietly, she said, "I'd like to buy you some food, if that's OK. How about a couple of burgers?"

The sentence was barely out of her mouth when he smoothly replied, "Well, I'd like to get her something a little more nutritious than that. Do you think you could just spare the cash?" He smiled at her shyly.

"Great," Penny thought. "Now what? I can't just walk away without helping to get this little kid something to eat, but I don't feel right handing this guy five bucks. What if he turns around and walks to the nearest liquor store? Katarín's right, though—I have no idea if that's a beer bottle in his pocket. But I don't even know if the little girl is his child, or if I'm being scammed."

"Miss? Could I have the money? Please?" the man pleaded.

Penny folded her hand around the bill in her pocket and said, " . . .

1. Do you think most people feel the same way Penny does about high school? Why or why not?
2. How does Penny feel about Community Service Day?
3. What makes Penny uncomfortable about working with the homeless?
4. How does Katarín feel about Penny's reaction to Community Service Day?
5. Why does Penny feel "a sudden surge of bravery" when she sees the man and the little girl?
6. How would you feel if you had Penny's Community Service assignment? How would you feel if you had Katarín's?

IIIII *THINKING ABOUT THE ENDING*

Penny must decide whether or not she believes that the man will use the money for food. She is concerned by the bottle in his pocket and her past experience with giving money to the homeless, but she feels strongly about getting some food for the man and the little girl. She also knows that her friend is watching to see what she will do. What, if anything, helps Penny to make her decision? Does she give the money to the man?

Using what you know about Penny, write an ending to the story in which Penny gives the money to the man and the girl, insists on buying the food herself, or walks away. Describe her thoughts as she makes her decision, as well as the reactions of the man, the little girl, and Katarín.

Polaroid

by Lottie E. Porch

For the past week, Ebony had secretly wanted to ask her mother about the photograph. She had found it hidden in an old book of poetry on the bookshelf. Normally, she didn't bother with the books in the living room, but relatives were coming for a long weekend, so Ebony decided to surprise her parents and clean the living room from top to bottom. When she went to dust the old books at the top of the high bookcase, the photograph fell out.

It was a small, faded, color snapshot of two people—Ebony's mother, Alean, and a man. From the looks in their eyes and the way they embraced, Ebony guessed that this man was her mother's old boyfriend.

Something in the man's face intrigued Ebony. Could she have seen him before? She doubted it. The clothes they wore reflected the time of the photo. Her mother's dress was purple with big white flowers. The man wore a gold knit sweater, and both had huge Afro hairstyles. The picture must have been taken sometime in the seventies, before Ebony was born.

No, Ebony couldn't know the man. Perhaps he just looked like someone she knew or had known. Still, she was intrigued and decided to find out more.

Ebony didn't feel quite right asking about this man in front of her dad and her other relatives. So she waited until the long holiday weekend was over and all the company was gone.

On Tuesday evening, when her dad was working late, Ebony approached her mother, who was alone in her room. Alean was relaxing and reading a magazine.

"Mom, guess what I found the other day?" Ebony asked.

"A million dollars," said her mother with a sly smile.

"No, you know if I had found that kind of money, I couldn't keep it to myself."

Alean put her magazine down. "Well then, I don't know. What did you find?"

"An old photo of you," said Ebony.

"Really?"

"I think you were with an old boyfriend."

"What are you talking about?" Alean looked concerned.

"Well, I don't know who he is really," admitted Ebony. "I guess he was your boyfriend. You did have a boyfriend before Daddy, didn't you?"

"Ebony, what is this all about?"

Ebony handed the picture to her mother. "You two sure look like you're in love," she said.

"Oh my goodness," Alean gasped, "Where did you find this?"

"In a dusty old book," replied her daughter. "What is it, Mom? You look upset."

Alean stared at the picture. For a moment, her eyes seemed glued to the man's face. When she looked back up at Ebony, her eyes mirrored a sadness the girl had only seen once before. When Ebony's uncle had died, her mother had cried like a child. Now, she looked ready to cry again.

"I'm sorry, Mom. I didn't mean to upset you," Ebony said. "It was just that I feel like I know this man somehow. Did I meet him a long time ago?"

"No, Ebony, you never met him."

"Well, who is he, Mom?" Ebony asked.

"It's a long story, Sweetheart."

Ebony was beginning to feel uneasy. "Mom, what do you mean?"

"I really don't know where to begin. I always meant to tell you, but the time never seemed right."

"Mom, what do you mean?" Ebony repeated.

"I mean," Alean stammered, "he's your father."

"What?" Ebony cried. "My father is at work. What is going on?"

"I'm talking about your biological father, not your adopted father," explained Alean.

"Adopted? You mean I'm adopted?"

"Yes."

Ebony stared at her mother in disbelief. Her voice became almost a whisper as she asked the next question. "Does this mean that you're not my mother?"

"No, Baby. I'm your mother," said Alean. "But the man in the picture is your daddy, not Louis."

"Mama, this is crazy. I remember Louis from the time I could talk. We have pictures of Louis and me from when I was a baby. How could he not be my father?"

As Alean struggled to find the words, Ebony suddenly knew why the man looked familiar. His face, with its smooth milk-chocolate skin, was the same as hers. They shared the same deep-set hazel eyes. In that instant, Ebony knew her mother was telling the truth.

Without blinking, she said, "Why didn't you tell me? I had a right to know."

"Of course you had a right to know. We just didn't know how to tell you."

"Well, who is he, Mama? Where is he?"

Alean's eyes were sad again, and they held a faraway look as if she were transported into the past. Struggling to explain, Alean began. "He was the first man I ever loved. I mean really loved. We met at the beginning of my sophomore year in college. He was a junior, but he was having a really hard time finding money to finish school. I was on a full scholarship, so I didn't have that pressure. Anyway, he was wonderful. He was gentle and loving, and he worked so hard. Occasionally, his temper would flare up, but other than that, he was perfect. But by the end of his junior year, he was too broke to continue. He had to drop out and get a job.

He got drafted right away, and I was devastated. The thought of him going to Vietnam was almost too much to bear. Anyway, about a week before he left, we went away together. We talked about getting married when he returned from the war. A month after he went to Vietnam, he was killed. I couldn't believe it, and then I found out you were on the way. I guess people wanted me to be ashamed, but I was happy. He was gone, but not totally because you were coming."

"What about Daddy—I mean, Louis?" Ebony asked. "How did he come into our lives?"

"I met Louis at college. We were always the best of friends," Alean explained. "He knew how broken up I was when your father died, and he stuck by me. I made a decision to have you and keep you. I dropped out of school for a year, and my parents had a fit. But Louis was there. After you came, he watched over you like you were his own. He loved you from the start. At first I didn't love him, but as time went by, my feelings changed. I was determined to finish college. When I graduated, he asked me to marry him. I knew he would be a good father, so we got married, and he adopted you."

"Mama, this is unbelievable. Everything I always thought about the two of you isn't true," said Ebony.

"Baby, I know we should have told you. We were just afraid."

The steely tone in Ebony's voice surprised them both. "Afraid of what, the truth? Did it ever occur to you that it might be important for me to know who my real father was?"

"We wanted to make sure you would be old enough to understand," said her mother.

"Mother, I'm 15. How old did I need to be?" asked Ebony. "In three years, I'll be on my own. I don't even know his name."

"His name was James Lee Harris," Alean replied, almost in a whisper.

"Harris?" Ebony cried. "You mean to tell me I could be related to Harrises all over this city, and not even know it?"

"Honey, you're getting upset. Now just calm down."

"You lied! Everybody knew about this big fat lie, except me." Ebony replied bitterly.

"Sweetheart, we love you. Surely, you know that."

"Well, Louis didn't have much choice, did he?" replied Ebony. "No, and neither do I."

In spite of her efforts to remain calm, Alean's voice was charged with emotion. "What are you talking about? I was the one left with no choice."

"Whose fault was that?" Ebony yelled.

"Don't you raise your voice at me, young lady," snapped Alean. "Who do you think you are?"

"Well, until about ten minutes ago, I thought I knew. Now, I really have no idea, do I?"

"Your temper is just like your father's," Alean said.

"Really?" Ebony shot back. "Which one?"

Before Alean knew what she was doing, her hand came down hard across Ebony's cheek. "You have no right to disrespect me like that! I'm still your mother!" she cried.

Ebony's eyes flashed pain and then disgust. Instantly, Alean was sorry. But Ebony was already out of the room and heading toward the door. As she reached for the knob, the door swung open. Ebony bumped headlong into Louis who announced, "I'm home." Ebony stared at him for a long moment and then said . . .

||||■ THINKING ABOUT THE STORY

1. What does Ebony learn from the photograph she finds?
2. How does Ebony react to the news?
3. Do you think her reaction is justified? Why or why not?
4. Is her mother's response justified? Explain.
5. Should Alean have revealed the past to Ebony? Why or why not?

||||■ THINKING ABOUT THE ENDING

How do you think Louis will react when he learns what has just happened? Will Ebony leave home or stay? Based on what you already know about Ebony, Alean, and Louis, write an ending that describes what Ebony says and does next.

Ash-Shahid— "The Witness"

by Joyce Haines

Chris Elkhart was finally getting used to the city. He could navigate his way through almost any town, day or night. What's more, Chris discovered that he could now walk through the darkest alleys without fearing for his life. He could then go back to a good meal, a warm room, and a soft bed. At last, his life—and his temper—seemed to be under control.

Chris had left the Lakota reservation at Pine Ridge, South Dakota, almost four years ago. Since Grandfather was gone, there was nothing left for Chris at home. He was only 17 at the time, but he felt as if he had lived forever. He was tired of trying to stay warm. He was tired of trying to stay out of trouble. He was tired of trying to survive one day at a time.

The Army recruiters in Rapid City didn't pay much attention to the shivering, gangly boy with the shadow of a black eye. He was fresh out of high school. He had no parents, no next of kin, and no prison record. The recruiters weren't worried. They knew that all he wanted was a warm, safe place to eat, sleep, and get some job training. It was a fair trade.

So Chris left Pine Ridge—one of the poorest reservations in the United States—and made his way in the world. He survived eight weeks of basic training in Fort Jackson, South Carolina, where he gained muscle as well as weight. Then he studied computers in Fort Huachuca, in Arizona. To relieve the strain on his eyes and shoulders, Chris often walked in the desert. It pleased him to know that the plant the natives of the area called "manzanita" was related to the "kinnikinnick" they used in prayer ceremonies back home. At the end of a long solitary walk in the desert, surrounded by the manzanita and the fragrant juniper, Chris was refreshed and ready to start again. Eventually, he began to bring back some juniper needles to burn each morning as he greeted the day, just as Grandfather had taught him.

Chris carried some juniper with him on his overseas assignment in Darmstadt, Germany. Military life was not easy at first, but after three years, Chris was promoted to sergeant and became a full-fledged Geographic Information Systems (GIS) analyst. He still couldn't believe that he'd been allowed to work with the most sophisticated computer mapping system in the world. Chris was using GIS and satellite images to locate water, mineral resources, and abandoned toxic-waste sites. He specialized in mapping water resources, in honor of Grandfather, who had taught him to respect this precious gift of life.

Chris thought that he had played it safe and smart. Now, he had an education and a good job skill. He had even managed to avoid fights. He had seen no armed combat at all. The past was over. He had cut all ties with Pine Ridge. No letters passed to or from his home. His Army buddies, with problems of their own, didn't ask questions, except for Mario, who was friendly to everyone.

The long hours Chris spent sitting in front of the GIS computer screen became a time when he could forget the violence of the past. His Army teachers called this "real time." Only now and then did Chris see reflected in the screen the angry faces of local gang lords. Somehow, he managed to erase the picture of their leader—the one who had called Chris a coward—and the fierce fight that followed that remark. Most of the time, the drone of the computer's fan brought Chris back to the chant of his grandfather, singing in the *Inipi*, the sweat-lodge purification ceremony.

The chant would last for hours. Yet, Grandfather would never bend down to avoid the stinging heat of the burning steam bath as he threw handfuls of water on the sacred rocks. He would never hide his face with a towel to avoid the steam. Other men crouched near the ground, moaning in pain. But Grandfather always sat with his back straight and his voice strong, chanting a special song to each of the four directions. At the end of every *Inipi*, Grandfather would speak a kind word to his quiet young grandson. "You have much courage," he would say.

These days, Chris preferred to be alone with his fond memories of Grandfather. He usually refused Mario's invitations to go into Darmstadt because he had heard that fights broke out when the parties got too rowdy.

"Come on, Chris. It's time for some R and R," Mario was saying. "You can't stare at that computer all the time. Hey, that's pretty cool. Did you design that cow grazing across your screen?"

"It's not a cow, Mario. It's a white buffalo," explained Chris. "They mean a lot to my people. Thanks for the offer, but I want to fix the kink in this system." Chris appreciated Mario's genuine good nature, but he had learned to be suspicious of other people.

Toward the end of his tour of duty, Chris began to plan for the future. "Maybe I'll move to Phoenix, Arizona, the place named after the dead bird that rose up from its own ashes," he thought. "The winters aren't too bad. People leave you alone. I can get work as a computer analyst. The future might turn out all right after all. One more month, and I'm free."

His office door burst open. It was Mario. "Did you hear the news?" he cried. "We're all being deployed to Saudi Arabia into Operation Desert Storm!" Mario couldn't wait to "see some action." He wasn't about to go home with nothing to show for his time in the Army except a passport stamped "Frankfurt."

Chris felt as if he would suffocate. He'd been able to get through basic training by telling himself that it was only temporary. He wouldn't have to hurt anyone. The Army had rules, after all. He didn't let himself think that he might have to enter combat. He intended to keep the vow he had made to himself when he left Pine Ridge. He'd chosen computer training as an extra precaution. Computer nerds wouldn't have to go anywhere near the action. "My job's got nothing to do with combat. You've made a mistake. . . ." Chris started to explain.

"Think again, man," replied Mario. "This is a high-tech war. Our Saudi friends want some technical assistance in tracking SCUD missile attacks. They think they can find Saddam with the help of our fancy GIS. They need you, Sergeant, because you're one of the best. We leave tonight."

The six-hour flight to Riyadh, Saudi Arabia, gave Chris time to think. "Well, I wanted to get away from the cold and the damp," he laughed to himself. "Grandfather always said to be careful what you ask for." Chris thought about Grandfather's small, drafty cabin with the old wood stove and the handmade star quilt on the bed. On the table sat an elkhide drum. Grandfather got it in a trade with a Cree who needed some red pipestone. Wrapped away was Grandfather's own sacred pipe, used only for the sundance and the *Inipi*.

The old man and the boy had taken many "sweats" together. Neither Chris's father nor his uncle were allowed to join in the community sweat-lodge ceremony after they returned from Vietnam. According to the Lakota tradition, the angry spirits of men killed in combat stay with their murderers forever. These spirits must not mingle with the good spirits invited into the lodge.

Sitting quietly in the liquid blackness of the sweat lodge, Chris could see only the dancing red and blue lights of the cedar needles that Grandfather placed gently onto the hot rocks before the water was brought in. Each dancing light of the embers seemed to hold a message for Chris.

When the time was right, Grandfather held a special *Inipi* for Chris, and then guided his vision quest on Bear

Butte. Many years ago, Grandfather had been a fierce warrior for his tribe. People still talked about his exploits. Yet, Grandfather began to lead Chris on a different path. During each of the four long nights of the vision quest, while Grandfather tended the small fire some distance away, Chris had heard the same voice. At first, Chris was too cold, too hungry, and too frightened to hear the voice clearly. Yet, each night, the voice became stronger, more clear. On the fourth night, the voice told him to be a man of peace. "Respect all life, even the rocks and trees. Even the enemy. *Mitakuye Oyasin*," the voice said. "We are all related." Chris was too ashamed to tell Grandfather about the enemies he had made at school, but as they walked back down Bear Butte together, Grandfather smiled in understanding when Chris described the voice.

A week after he arrived in Saudi Arabia, Chris was still thinking about Grandfather and the Spirit voice. While he traveled across the desert in the Army jeep, the faint aroma of smoking cedar and sweetgrass seemed to purify the air. After being away four years, Chris knew that it was time to visit Bear Butte for a little while before he started his new life.

Chris was suddenly brought back to the present by a rising dust storm that came out of nowhere. "Where's the road?" shouted the driver as the jeep came to a halt. He cursed and jumped out to clean the air filter. They had passed into Iraq hours ago. The Iraqi army could be anywhere. It was getting darker by the minute. "We should have been in Basra by now. Where are we?" asked their leader, Lieutenant Garcia.

Chris studied the map. "We're about to enter a village called *Ash-Shahid*. It means "the witness"—one of the 99 names of their Great Spirit, Allah." The reverence of Arabic place names impressed Chris. The *Al Rashid* Hotel in Baghdad meant "the guide to the right path," another name of Allah. His own name, *Elkhart*, referred to the courageous heart of one of the Native Americans' most respected animals.

Chris had also heard that some Arabs would repeat one phrase a thousand times a day, *La il la ha, il Alla hu* ("There is no God but God"). He understood that this was their way of remembering the Great Spirit. He thought Grandfather would like that. He could almost hear their chanting, sung to the beat of a Native American drum.

"Sshhh!" motioned Lieutenant Garcia. He nudged the driver. "Wait. There's something out there." The journalist traveling with them didn't say a word. Every muscle of his face and shoulders was as tight as the elk skin stretched over Grandfather's drum. Moments before, he and Lieutenant Garcia had been trading stories about their courageous exploits in Baghdad. They had also discussed the mass starvation among the Iraqi soldiers. Most were in no condition to fight. Everywhere, entire platoons of soldiers were surrendering. They had been abandoned by their leader, left to starve in the desert. But a few had been known to fight to the death when the U.S. Army found them. Garcia himself had killed at least 12 of them, he told the journalist.

"That noise. I heard it, too," said Chris.

"Let's get out of here," whispered the journalist. The wind had shifted. The air was very still. Just as the driver was getting back behind the wheel, Garcia noticed the Iraqi crawling by a camouflaged tank 25 yards away. The journalist dove face down onto the car floor, flinging his hands over his head.

"Wait. What about taking prisoners?" Chris demanded as Garcia lunged for the box of grenades.

"This is war, Elkhart," Garcia snarled. "It's us or them. Do you think they would give *us* a chance?"

"But, but . . ." Chris stammered. No one could guess how many soldiers might be in the area or what their physical condition might be. Yet, even from a distance, Chris could sense no threat coming from the Iraqi. His deep brown eyes reminded Chris of the eyes of his cousins. Once again, Chris heard the old Spirit Voice ringing inside his head. "*Mitakuye Oyasin.* We are all related," the voice spoke, followed by the name, *Ash-Shahid*—"the witness."

Turning around to face his commanding officer, Chris spoke, "There's no reason to kill him, Lieutenant."

"What's the matter Elkhart? Are you afraid to shed a little blood? I'm ordering you to shoot, soldier. Do you want to leave the Army with a clean record or a dishonorable discharge? What are you going to do?"

Chris looked at Garcia and then at the Iraqi. Then he made his decision. He . . .

1. Why did Chris join the Army?
2. Describe Chris's relationship with his grandfather.
3. What did Chris experience on his vision quest?
4. How was his vision quest important to him?
5. Why does Chris notice the Arabic names?
6. Why does Chris hesitate to obey Lieutenant Garcia's order?

|||■ *THINKING ABOUT THE ENDING*

Chris is looking forward to a good civilian job after his discharge from the Army. But he is faced with a conflict. He must decide whether to obey his commanding officer or his own conscience. Think about what Chris learned from his vision quest and the sweat-lodge purifications he took with his grandfather. Do you think he will obey the lieutenant's orders to kill the Iraqi? Why or why not? Write an ending to this story that describes what Chris thinks and does in response to the lieutenant's orders.

Fourth Down and Ten

by Wiley M. Woodard

The bitter November wind whipped through the trees outside Marvin's bedroom window. The leaves had changed to red and gold some time ago. This time of year always made Marvin think of football.

Ever since he was a little boy, Marvin loved football. He played the game whenever and wherever he could. He played with his friends in the park that was just two blocks from where he lived. He played on a local football team as a kid. It came as no surprise to anyone that when he began Central High School, Marvin tried out for the football team.

Marvin played tackle on the team. It wasn't long before he was assigned to play quarterback. That was the position he wanted to play more than anything.

Then a knee injury during a Central–Southside game put an end to Marvin's gridiron glory. He'd thrown a great pass—he'd waited for the right receiver to be open. He saw the pass completed and watched the receiver head for the end zone. Then—bang—he was hit from behind. He never saw the guy coming.

The doctor warned Marvin not to play football again. If he did, he might hurt his knee permanently. Because Marvin was no longer able to play sports, he decided to write about them. He began to write for the school paper's sports section.

As the wind made a faint whistling sound outside, Marvin continued to think about the game. He recalled

Coach Chen's words after that last game: "You are one of our best players, Marvin. However, your health is more important than any team. If there is anything I can do, please let me know."

Marvin really admired Coach Chen. The coach didn't believe in grandstand players. Playing the best game you could, and playing fair, was more important to him. It made Coach Chen beam with pride when his team won a game because they played hard and fair.

Marvin was so lost in thought that he didn't hear Marissa and Carlos enter his room. Marissa was the editor of the school newspaper. She and Marvin had been friends since grade school. Carlos was Marvin's best friend.

"*Qué pasa, mi amigo?*" Carlos asked.

Marvin looked up, surprised to see his two friends. "Hey, guys," he responded.

"Your mother said it was OK for us to come up," Marissa said.

"What brings you two here?" Marvin asked.

"We wanted to drop by and see how our favorite sports writer is doing," Marissa replied.

"You mean your *only* sports writer," grinned Marvin.

"The staff loved your story on the new uniforms," said Marissa. "Now all we need is your story on the city championship football game. Our winning would be the best retirement present we could give Coach Chen."

Marvin noticed a pained look cross Carlos's face.

"That shouldn't be a hard story to write. Our team has been terrific lately, like in that game against Southside," said Marvin.

"Right. Wouldn't it be great if we won the city championship?" Marissa exclaimed.

"They can do it, too," smiled Marvin, "even without their all-time star quarterback."

"You deserve some of the credit," said Carlos quietly. "Before your knee injury, you helped turn the Central High football team into winners."

"I think most of the credit goes to Coach Chen," Marvin added. "He's a coach and a good friend to a lot of the guys. I think they play hard because they don't want to let him down. He believed in the team when we didn't believe in ourselves."

"Let's not forget our offensive line. They're playing stronger than ever," offered Marissa.

Marvin and Carlos looked at each other with surprise. Marissa had never quite cared for football until this past season. She used to argue that the sport was too aggressive. Now she'd become Central High's number-one football fan.

"Maybe you should write the story about the football game this afternoon," said Marvin.

"I couldn't write the story as well as you can," said Marissa.

"I wouldn't have thought so either, a while ago. Now, I'm not so sure," Marvin said.

Marissa smiled. "Well, we'd better be off if you wrote it," she said. "Carlos and I are studying together at the library."

"I want to talk Marvin a little longer. Why don't you go ahead, Marissa? I'll meet you at the library in a while," Carlos said.

"OK. See you later at the game, Marvin," Marissa said. She waved goodbye and was out the door.

"Is everything OK, Carlos? Looks like there's something on your mind. What gives?" Marvin asked.

"I've been thinking a lot about something lately. I think I should talk to you about it," Carlos said.

"What's up, buddy?" Marvin asked.

"A couple of the guys from our team have been sneaking into Southside's locker room and copying Southside's plays," Carlos said.

"How do you know?" Marvin asked.

"Ted Jones, the quarterback who took your place on the team, told me. He made me promise not to tell anyone," said Carlos.

"Are you sure he's not lying?" Marvin asked.

"I wouldn't be telling you if I wasn't sure," Carlos replied.

"Central and Southside have been rivals for a long time. Maybe Central is playing better because Coach Chen and the team are used to the way Southside plays," offered Marvin.

"Central has a real good team. Maybe we got to the city championship on our own skill—this is the last game of the season, so we'll never know. But Ted says that our team is there, playing last year's champs, because we stole plays from their playbooks," said Carlos.

"Coach Chen would be furious if he heard about this," said Marvin. "I really wish you hadn't told me."

"What do you mean if Coach Chen ever heard about this?" Carlos asked.

"This is his last game as coach before he retires. His team finally has a chance to be the champs," said Marvin.

"What do you think we should do? If we tell him, he'll feel like a failure because the guys cheated. If we don't tell him, it's as good as helping them cheat," Carlos said.

Marvin thought hard for a minute. Then he said . . .

IIIII THINKING ABOUT THE STORY

1. How does Marvin feel about Coach Chen?

2. Why is the city championship so important to Central High School?

3. Why do you think the Central players are stealing plays from the other team?

4. Why does Carlos betray Ted's confidence and tell Marvin about the stolen plays?

5. How do you think Coach Chen would feel if he found out what his team has done?

||||■ THINKING ABOUT THE ENDING

Marvin wants to see Coach Chen rewarded for his hard work by having Central win the city championship before he retires. However, he knows that stealing the playbook goes against every value Coach Chen tried to instill in his team. What do you think he decides to do?

Use what you have learned about Marvin and Coach Chen to write an ending in which Marvin ignores the news Carlos shares with him or tells Coach Chen before the city championship game. You might also think of another choice Marvin could make. Describe Marvin's thoughts as well as the action you think he will take.

The Noodle-Shop Incident

by Kipp Erante Cheng

I spent the summer after graduating from high school working at a weekly news magazine in New York City. It was an entry level position, but I felt that the experience would be useful in the future and help me with my writing skills before I entered college.

One day, I went to work expecting nothing unusual to happen. I picked up a cup of coffee at the corner coffee shop and a copy of the morning paper at the newsstand. When I got to work, I saw a note on my desk asking me to see my boss, Mr. Hinckle, as soon as I got in. Mr. Hinckle often told me that I was doing a good job and that my writing was improving. I appreciated everything he did for me, especially hiring me for the summer, even though I had little news experience.

I put my coffee and newspaper down on my desk and sat down to catch my breath before I went into Mr. Hinckle's office. For all I knew, he was planning to fire me and I would be out of a job by lunchtime. I tried not to think about that possibility. Instead, I tried to focus on all the good work I had done at the magazine and the praise I had received since I came on board. It's not often that a young Japanese American woman can make it in this business. I was proud to be one of those who had succeeded.

I went to Mr. Hinckle's office and saw that the door was open. He was sitting at his desk, with the telephone receiver in the crook of his neck. He motioned for me to enter.

"Can you wait a minute for me to finish this call?" Mr. Hinckle asked, covering the mouthpiece with his hand.

"Of course," I said, fidgeting a little in the chair in front of his desk.

Mr. Hinckle continued his phone call, laughing occasionally at a joke or comment from the person on the other side of the line. After what seemed like forever, Mr. Hinckle hung up the telephone and stared at me.

"Tell me how long you've been with this magazine, Miss Tanaka," he finally said.

"About six weeks, sir," I replied.

"Hired you right after graduation, didn't we?" he asked.

"Yes, sir."

Mr. Hinckle smiled and a sudden wave of panic surged through my entire body.

"Listen, Jennifer, you don't have to call me Mr. Hinckle or Sir. If I can call you Jennifer, then you should call me Sam."

"All right," I said, suddenly feeling a lot better.

"Listen, Jennifer, I called you into my office this morning for a reason."

"Oh?" Again I felt a wave of panic.

"You see, we're planning to make a few personnel changes at the office and . . ."

My heart sank to the pit of my stomach. Mr. Hinckle was going to fire me! What a way to begin the week. I sat in silence and watched his lips move, but I didn't understand a word he said until he finished his sentence.

" . . . so that's what I wanted to tell you this morning," Mr. Hinckle said. "You can move to the bigger desk, closer to my office."

I looked at Mr. Hinckle, astonished.

"Is there something wrong, Jennifer?"

"It's just . . . . " I couldn't finish my sentence.

"What is it?" Mr. Hinckle asked again.

"Did you just fire me, Mr. Hinckle?"

Mr. Hinckle began to laugh. "Are you kidding?" he said.

"I just gave you a promotion. You're going to be the new researcher for my staff. This new position will definitely help your writing skills before you head off for college. Congratulations, Jennifer."

"I don't know what to say. Thank you so much, Mr. Hin—I mean, Sam."

"You're very welcome, Jennifer. You deserve this promotion. Now get back to work." Mr. Hinckle smiled at me, and I went back to my desk. I sat and looked around at the small cubicle that used to be my office. It had been my home for six weeks, and I felt sad about leaving it. But then I started to think about my new position and all the responsibilities that I would have. I thought about how much faith Mr. Hinckle must have in me to give me a promotion. Suddenly, I felt very secure and happy with my summer job.

My friend Jack was working at another magazine a few blocks away. Because we would be going to the same college in the fall, I thought he would appreciate the news about my promotion. I called him after I moved to my new and bigger desk.

"You won't believe what happened to me this morning," I said, trying to contain my excitement.

"What, Jenn?" Jack asked.

"Mr. Hink—I mean Sam gave me a promotion this morning. I'm calling from my big new desk that's near a window overlooking Central Park."

"I can't believe it," Jack said. "I'm so happy for you. We'll have to celebrate. How about if we meet for lunch?"

"Sounds good to me," I said.

"Let's meet at the Chinese noodle shop on the corner," Jack said, "How about 12:30?"

"Sounds great. See you then."

"Bye, Jenn," Jack said, "and congratulations."

After I got off the telephone, I went into Sam's office to tell him that I was going to take a longer lunch than usual.

"Take as long as you like," Mr. Hinckle said. "You should celebrate today."

"Thanks, Sam," I said, too happy to contain myself.

As I walked down Seventh Avenue, I thought there was nothing in the world that could bring me down.

I arrived at the noodle shop several minutes early. I enjoyed sitting in the waiting area, looking at the pretty decorations in the restaurant, and watching the waiter pass by with platters of delicious food. The manager smiled at me and asked if I would like to be seated, but I said, "I'm waiting for a friend. He'll be here any minute."

I waited for 15 minutes and still no Jack. I went to the telephone and called his office, but the receptionist said that he had already left. I was relieved to know that Jack was on his way. I was beginning to feel really hungry.

I sat down once again and looked through a magazine I had in my backpack. As I was flipping through the pages, I felt a tap on my shoulder. I looked up to see an unfamiliar man standing in front of me.

"Excuse me," he said, very slowly, as if he was trying to make each word as clear as possible. "Do you have a telephone in the restaurant?"

"What?" I said, confused by the man's question.

"I said, do you have a telephone in this restaurant," he

repeated. "Don't you speak English?"

A wave of rage ran through my body. "Of course I speak English. Do you?" I said.

"Aren't you from China?" he said.

"No, I am not from China," I snapped back. "Would you mind leaving me alone?"

"All of you Chinks are the same," he said, "You all think that you're better than the rest of us. At least, I don't work in a restaurant."

"I'm sorry, sir, but I don't work in a restaurant either," I said, standing up and trying to get away.

"All of you Chinks work in restaurants, don't you?" he said. By now I realized he was very drunk.

"No. We don't all work in restaurants. Besides, I'm not Chinese. I'm Japanese. Japanese American."

"Japanese, Chinese—what's the difference?" he said. "You're all the same."

This man had the most vacant blue eyes I had ever seen. He smirked at me, and it took all the strength I could muster to keep from slapping his face. I thought about calling the police, but I felt as if the man had me cornered. It made me so angry that he was picking on me just because I looked Asian and I was in a Chinese restaurant. I was angry that other patrons in the restaurant just turned away, doing nothing to help me. I was angry that Jack was so late.

The manager saw what was happening and came over to help.

"Are you all right, young lady?" he asked me.

"As a matter of fact," I said, "I'm not all right. This man is harassing me."

"I'm not harassing her," the drunk man said. "She's a friend of mine."

"I'm not his friend," I insisted, but the drunk grabbed my arm and pulled me toward him.

"Don't you want to give me a kiss?" he asked, as I tried to push him away.

I suddenly felt as if I were out of my body, watching this scene from somewhere above my head. There I was, struggling to get away from this drunk, while the restaurant manager and several waiters tried to pull him away from me. Then, from out of the corner of my eye, I saw Jack enter the restaurant.

"What's going on here?" Jack shouted.

"Jack!" I said, struggling to get away.

I saw the drunk lurch toward Jack, swinging his right arm at Jack's face. Jack ducked and moved away before the man could hit him. The man lost his footing, stumbled to the ground, and passed out on the floor. I looked at Jack, who stood there in disbelief, and then at the crowd that had gathered around us. I looked at all these people and completely forgot about the great day I was having. I forgot about the promotion and Mr. Hinckle. I forgot about my morning walk to work. I forgot about the coffee and the newspaper from the newsstand. I forgot about all these things, and I just stared out into the crowd of faces staring back at me.

"Jenn?" Jack said. "Are you all right? Jenn, can you hear me?"

"Yeah," I said.

"I'm sorry I was late, Jenn," Jack said. "What do you want to do?"

"What do you mean?" I asked.

"Do you want to press charges?" Jack said. "We could get the cops to put the guy in jail where he belongs."

"I don't know, Jack," I said.

"Jenn, this guy deserves to be taught a lesson," Jack said. "If he did it to you, he could do it to someone else."

I thought for a moment. Jack was right. I had been harassed—and even assaulted. But if I pressed charges against him, I would have to go to court and testify. Then this incident would drag out for a long time. I just wanted to forget about the whole thing. But I felt awful about letting this man get away with his actions. Finally, I decided.

"Jack," I said, "I'm going to . . . "

IIII■ THINKING ABOUT THE STORY

1. Describe Jennifer's expectations for the day she thinks she is going to have.

2. How do Jennifer's expectations of her meeting with Mr. Hinckle differ from what really happens?

3. How is the celebration of Jennifer's promotion ruined at the restaurant?

4. What does the drunk at the restaurant do to provoke Jennifer? Do you think he means to harass her? Explain.

5. How does Jennifer's perception of her "ordinary" day change by the time Jack arrives at the restaurant?

IIII■ THINKING ABOUT THE ENDING

Jennifer does not expect to receive the promotion at her job, but she happily accepts it. When she calls Jack to celebrate, she can't anticipate the incident at the restaurant. What choices does she have to make in order to get the drunk to leave her alone? How does the crowd of people around her react? What does Jack do to stop the incident from going any further?

By the end of the incident, Jennifer's great day has become a pretty awful one. Write an ending in which she decides what to do and how that decision affects her.

*J*im Hill's Dream

by James Bruchac

Jim Hill and Larry Jackson stood waiting for the subway to take them to the park.

"Man, I can't take this heat today," Jim said, wiping the sweat off his forehead.

"I don't know what's worse, the heat or the smell of this place. I hate the subway in August," Larry said. A moment later, the subway arrived, and Jim and Larry grabbed two seats. Ten minutes later, they were walking the two blocks to the park.

"So, Jim, you still got that crazy idea of playing football?" Larry asked as they walked. "Practice starts tomorrow, doesn't it?"

Jim hesitated. "Sure I'm going to do it," he said. "It's either now or never." Jim tried to hide his nervousness. He had trained all summer for his first season of football, and practice started tomorrow.

"You'd better get used to the heat, Jimmy boy. I hear Coach Long works his team till they drop, without even a water break," Larry said.

"It couldn't get any hotter than my grandfather's sweat lodge," Jim said with a smile.

"What's a sweat lodge?" Larry asked.

Jim explained a Native American sweat lodge as simply as he could. He told Larry that it was like a church because you prayed a lot—for yourself, other people in the lodge, the earth, future generations, or anything else you felt the need to pray for. He explained how the red-hot rocks in the middle of the lodge brought you closer to the earth and helped burn away impurities.

"How do you feel afterward?" Larry asked.

"Like a newborn baby," Jim answered.

He thought back to the time he had seen his grandfather two summers ago. Every other year, Jim and his family visited his grandparents in the country. His grandfather was with him the first time he was in a sweat lodge. He told Jim the stories of his Native American ancestors. They were often amusing, but they also taught lessons and told of bravery, overcoming great odds, and finding the strength within your heart to meet any challenge.

The stories encouraged Jim to finally try out for the football team. His friends said he was too small to play football, but he had gained 15 pounds over the last year and had grown to over 6 feet. They still tried to discourage him, though, saying it was too late to try out for a new sport in his junior year.

"All the good players started in grade school. If you even make the team, you'll just sit on the bench," one friend had said.

Jim tried hard to ignore the comments, but they were always in the back of his mind. He knew it would be hard to start playing football at his age, but he was determined to try.

As Tamara and Amanda, the boys' girlfriends, approached, Larry said, "Well, today is Jim's last day before he starts football—his last day of summer and freedom." He gave Jim a light punch in the arm.

"I think it's great that Jim's trying out for the team," said Amanda.

"As long as he stays in one piece," said Tamara.

Jim smiled and took Tamara's hand as they walked toward the pond at the center of the park. Jim knew it was his last day of relaxation for a while, and he cherished every moment of it.

Early the next morning, Jim headed over to the football locker room for the first pre-season meeting. As he approached the gym, he began to doubt his decision.

"This is crazy," he said to himself. He paused for a moment, realizing that all he had to do was turn around and go home. But he thought of a story he had been told as a child, the story of the seventh direction. In the story, after the places of the six directions in the world were given—North, South, East, West, Sky, and Earth—the animals had to decide where to hide the most powerful of all directions, the seventh direction. This direction was the most powerful because anyone who discovered it could never truly be defeated.

After many animals had made suggestions, it was decided that the best place to hide the seventh direction was within the human heart because it was the last place most people would look. When found, its power would be unstoppable. As Jim remembered this lesson, he thought of that strength within his own heart and how important it was for him to try out for the team.

"This is it. My last chance at a dream. I can't give up now," he thought as he continued toward the building.

Walking into the locker room, Jim felt as if all eyes were upon him. Everyone was seated, waiting for the coaches. Jim swallowed and sat in the back of the room.

When Coach Long walked into the room, all conversation stopped. Standing 6-foot-4 and weighing over 200 pounds, he commanded respect.

"All right, boys, let's start with a roll call," Coach Long said. After every person had given his name, they went outside for the first pre-season test. During the first half of the day, everyone was tested in the 40-yard dash and the one-mile run. After lunch, they were tested in the bench press and squat.

Although it was a hot, humid day, Jim tested well, running the 40-yard dash in 4.7 seconds. After the last test, he rested on a bench outside the locker room. One of the assistant coaches walked up to him.

"I'm Coach Simmons, the defensive line coach. We could use some more boys at defensive end, especially someone with your speed," he said.

Jim talked to Coach Simmons for several minutes. He agreed to try out for a defensive end position. As he headed home, he thought about how well he had done.

"Nothing can stop me now," Jim said to himself as he neared his apartment.

That night, Jim talked with Tamara and Larry. He told them how well his first day had gone. Jim couldn't help bragging a little, especially to Larry, who had seemed to doubt his chances the most. After talking with his friends, Jim went to bed early so he'd be well rested for the next day of practice.

When he awoke the next morning, every muscle in his body ached. He felt as if he could barely get out of bed. Checking the clock, he saw that he had to be on the practice field in 30 minutes.

"How can I practice when it hurts to move?" Jim asked himself.

Another five minutes went by. Jim lay there thinking about how all his friends would probably be in bed for at least another hour and then have a relaxing day. But just as his doubts were growing, he remembered what he had learned from the old legends about fighting pain and fear. He remembered the story of the young man who defeated the cannibal giant. The young hero had to fight his fears and endure much pain. Many times he thought of giving up. Only after enduring it all and sticking to his task did the hero out-wit the cannibal giant and save his village. Jim also remembered how well he had done the day before and how Coach Simmons had noticed him.

"Better get up and at it," Jim thought as he threw the covers off, got dressed, and headed to morning practice.

At the beginning of practice, everyone was divided by positions. Jim went with the defensive linemen. All morning, they did position drills and practiced stances, pass rushing, and different defenses. Jim felt overwhelmed as the only first-year player on the defensive line. Though Coach Simmons did his best to give him extra help, Jim realized he was far behind the other players.

Afternoon practice was just as hard. Toward the end of the day, Coach Long had everyone run 12 40-yard dashes with only a 10-second break between each one. Jim's legs were so sore that he could barely walk back to the locker room.

The next two days of double-session practices were filled with more of the same. Though Jim was slowly learning his potential position, he felt more and more unsure about his decision. Every morning, it seemed harder and harder to get out of bed. Every night, when he talked to his friends, he would hear about how much they were enjoying the summer.

"Boy, Jim, you missed a great party yesterday," Larry said after Jim's second day of practice.

"Sure did miss being with you at the park today," Tamara said after Jim's third practice.

Even though Tamara and his other friends tried to encourage him, Jim began to think more and more about what he was missing.

On the fourth morning before practice, Jim almost decided he had had enough. He was working his hardest and was still way behind the other players at his position.

"I can't take this anymore," Jim said to himself as he lay in bed, watching the minutes tick by. Then, as before, he thought of the stories and teachings of the Native American legends. Jim thought once again of the sweat lodge and of the strength it took him to make it through his first time. He thought of how the heat had seemed to be more than he could bear and how he found the strength inside himself to go on. He remembered the story of the seventh direction and the power found within one's own heart.

"Just three more days of double sessions. I can make

it," Jim said to himself as he stood up to prepare for another day of practice.

Although he still had his doubts, Jim's practice that day seemed better than the earlier ones. He had done well enough to make it through the last cut before helmets and pads. As he sat in the locker room after the other players left for the day, Jim was fully aware of how much smaller he was than some of the offensive linemen he would have to face. They would be like those giants in the old stories.

"Giants were defeated by smaller men in legends, but these giants are real," Jim said to himself.

He felt a cold chill go up his spine when he thought of getting hit by those real giants time and time again. He thought of all the determination it had taken him just to make it through the last four days. The next three days would be the hardest, and he still had to make the final cut. Jim thought once again of Tamara, Larry, and his other friends enjoying the last days of summer before school started. He remembered an end-of-the-summer party Larry had told him about. He thought of all the other things he would miss throughout the school year, if he made the last cut. He would have to go to practice every day after school, be in early every Friday night before games, and travel every other weekend, sometimes getting back late at night. All this would take time away from Tamara and his other friends, as well as from his schoolwork.

That night, Tamara went to visit Jim. He told her his fears.

"Jim, you've done great! Everyone heard that you made the first cut," Tamara said.

"I guess I can't quit then. If I quit, I'll let everyone down," Jim responded.

"If you want to stop now, no one will blame you. Everyone knows how tough it's been. Besides, you don't have to prove anything to anybody except yourself," Tamara said.

Jim thought hard about his decision. He thought about all he had gone through so far to make the first cut and of the courage he had already found within himself. But he also remembered all the things he would miss and the great physical challenge that lay ahead. Last, he thought about what Tamara had said about not having to prove anything to anybody but himself. At that moment, Jim made his decision.

Turning to Tamara, Jim said, "Tamara, I've thought it over, and I've decided . . .

▍▍▍▍THINKING ABOUT THE STORY

1. What does Jim Hill dream of doing?

2. What difficulties in fulfilling this dream does he face in the story?

3. How does Jim deal with these difficulties?

4. What things will Jim miss if he continues to play football?

5. What does Tamara mean when she says that Jim only has to prove things to himself?

Jim Hill is faced with the difficult decision of whether to continue with his dream of playing football or to enjoy the rest of the summer and have more time during the school year for other things. What thoughts and fears are going through his head as he decides what to do? What do you think he tells Tamara?

Think back to what you learned about the challenges Jim must face. With that in mind, write an ending to the story in which Jim either continues with football or quits to have more time for his friends and schoolwork.

Mockingbird

by Cecilia Rubino

My name is Compton. I was born in Kingston, Jamaica. I live now at 427 President Street, at the corner of President and Utica. I live with my mother and two of my brothers. My mother's name is Marie Thomas. I am the second oldest in my family. I am 5 feet 8 inches tall. I have black hair, brown eyes, and one tooth in front that needs fixing. Everybody says I have a trusting face. Maybe so. But I tell people, "Don't trust me because I don't trust myself." I came up here a year ago, but I did not start school until January.

I don't have any more to write. I don't like writing. Usually, it doesn't sound right or say what I want to say. I am having some problems in my English class and in math, so they sent me for tutoring during third period. Everybody was teasing me in Room 123 about this red flower I have inside my jacket today. The girls say I have a secret valentine. But this rose is not from a girl. When I put on my coat this morning, I found this rose in my inside pocket with a card from my mom.

February 15

Compton,

You write really well! I'm Julia, one of the tutors here in

Room 123. I'm in college, but I come to your school in the mornings to help kids with English. There are also people here who can help you with math. It would be great if you could come down during third period. We usually start each session with some journal writing. Writing seems to clear the air and focus everybody. You can share your writing or keep it private. If you want me to write back in your journal, I will. It can be what we call a dialogue journal. That's like talking back and forth on paper. Don't worry about spelling and grammar; just write! Why did you wait until January to start school? I was very impressed that the rose was from your mom. She must love you very much.

February 16

My mother is the most important person in my life. My mother is the reason I am here. I did not start school when I first came because I had some things to take care of. I needed some clothes, and I was not ready. You said you wanted to know something about me. I will tell you. I hate this school. This school is no good for me. I didn't like school back home. Here, it is worse. You said you are in college and come here to work with kids because you like it. If I was in college, I would not come here. To me, this school looks like a prison. There is a security guard in every hall, and still the kids are too wild. I would not come here if I did not have to.

My mother wants me to have a diploma. That is why I cannot quit. She says you are not recognized in this country unless you have a diploma. But I think this is not a good school. Years ago, I dreamed of going to an American school. I would like the teachers, the clean classrooms, and the organized schedule. This school is a garbage dump. It needs to be fixed in so many places that I cannot count them all!

I had my transcripts from back home when I arrived, and the counselor still put me back a year. The system here drives me nuts. I received my program card, and the classes I want are not there. Now tell me, isn't education for us students to choose? This school has no communication, no discipline, and no organization.

What I want is to take a computer class. With computers, I can get a job where I can come home and not have to take a shower and change all my clothes. But they say that the computer courses are filled, and I need to study other things. So now I am having problems with math. I was good in math back home. Here, they do things completely different. But my math teacher is nice. She told me to come down and get help in the tutoring room.

My other big problem is English. Back home, English is just a subject. I was good at English. But I cannot understand the way the kids talk here. I get a headache listening to their English all day.

My English teacher is the biggest problem for me. He does everything so fast. I do not understand this teacher. He is Mr. Childs in 405. He combs his hair over the top of his bald head. I do not understand his accent or the books we have to read. We have tests in his class, and sometimes I have no idea what I am supposed to write. Now, I am supposed to choose between two books. *Of Mice and Men* is about a man who does not understand things. *To Kill a Mockingbird* is about racism. This is good, but I think this book is too hard for me. Mr. Childs says I don't try hard enough. He says I spoke English in Jamaica and that lots of kids who pass his test don't speak English at home. He says I will not pass his class if I don't do the work. This teacher does not like me.

I don't know what I am supposed to write about now. I don't write very well, but you can read it if you want. I don't care.

Compton,

Please tell me if I talk too fast for you, OK? It must be very hard for you coming in the middle of the year to this big, confusing school. Even I get confused here. Your English teacher probably does not realize that you don't speak English at home. You speak Creole, right? I'd be happy to work on *To Kill a Mockingbird* with you. This is a book I really love! It was one of those books that changed my life when I was in high school. But I can understand that it might be hard for someone who is not from here. Let's look at it together, and maybe we can go up and talk to Mr. Childs about what's going on in his class.

Compton, don't worry about your writing. You write really well! Look at how many pages you wrote in just ten minutes. Just remember that this journal is for writing anything that comes into your head. You can write about what you love the most or what you hate in this world. Write about what life was like back home or a dream you had last night, about what your goals are, or about what makes you really angry. Just keep writing!

I cannot write about what makes me angry. I don't want to get into that. If I wrote about that, I would write and write and never stop. My thoughts go too fast. I just want to be able to say it to the person. But most times, I just walk away.

Yesterday, I came home and my father was sitting on my couch. I couldn't believe it. I turned around and walked back out. My father came here because he wants me to go back home to Jamaica. He has money, but he doesn't share any of it with us. He abandoned my mother and did not give her any of his money. When I was growing up, we didn't have anything. My mother didn't even have money for sneakers to send us to school. Every year we would get these kind of sneakers that we called Rejects. They were very cheap and ugly. Sometimes, I was so embarrassed that I would put my church shoes on, just so other kids could not see I did not have good sneakers. When my mother came here, I went to stay with my father and this other woman he lives with. She takes all his money. He was so cheap; he wouldn't buy us anything. Nothing I did pleased him. Sometimes, I think my dad's gone crazy or is on drugs or something. He used to come home and pick on us all the time. He got mad at everybody. I tried to fight him, but he is too crazy. I ran away two times, but he brought me back.

Finally, my mother got money for airplane tickets. She had to trick him. My father thought my brothers and I were coming up here for vacation. But I am not going back. I can't believe my mother let him in her house.

This is the problem I have with the book *To Kill a Mockingbird*. I started this book. I have to look up a lot of words, but it's not too bad. I understand Scout, the girl, but I cannot relate to the father. He is like a saint. To me, this is not believable. My father is nothing like this at all. I don't ever want to see him again.

February 21

Compton,

It sounds like you have every reason in the world to be angry with your father. You know, you might want to think about writing a letter to him. Say all the things you want to say to him. Tell him why you don't want anything to do with him. You don't even have to send it. You can burn it, throw it away, or keep it to read ten years from now. But this is one of the things that I've been doing in my own journal. I write stuff to people whom I can't talk to directly because it helps me to get it out and work it through. I guess it makes me feel cleaner inside. Just think about it.

March 15

Dear Julia,

You know that part in *Mockingbird* where the brother, Jem, gets really mad at that racist lady? He knows she is stupid, ignorant, and sick, but he goes crazy and smashes up her garden.

I have a big problem. In Mr. Childs's class, we had a *Mockingbird* test the other day. I wrote all the answers, and it was good. So yesterday, he gave me back the paper. I had been writing fast, so I put my name in the margin on the side. But he knew it was my paper! On top of the paper, he put a big red x and wrote, "No name, no date, no grade." On the bottom, he put, "The next time you hand in a paper without a proper heading, it goes in the garbage!"

I walked right out. I was so mad I left my coat on the back of my chair. If I had stayed, I would have cursed that man out. But I had to go back and get my coat. When I came back everyone was out of the room, and I did a bad thing. You know that fire on the fourth floor yesterday? I started that fire. I guess I got a little crazy. I had a pack of matches. I lit them and threw them into that closet where he keeps all his extra paperbacks of that *Mockingbird* book.

Compton,

What Mr. Childs did may not be right, but setting books on fire doesn't help anybody. Thank God that the whole school didn't burn down. When Jem in *Mockingbird* gets in trouble for messing up that lady's garden, his father makes him go back. Even though the woman is a racist, his dad makes Jem apologize and pay for the damages by helping her out.

Compton, I don't really know why you told me this. I know I told you that you could write anything that came into your head in this journal. I don't want to betray your confidence. But I feel I'm in a strange position now. I don't think I'll feel right if I keep what I know about this fire a secret. But I understand that you were very angry, and that's why it happened. I don't want you to be upset with me if I talk to someone else about this. I feel like I should talk to the principal. But I don't want you to think I'm just turning you in. Maybe we could go together to explain what happened to Mr. Childs, or we could meet with your counselor. Let's find a place to talk. I hope we can figure this out. Right now, I really don't know what I should do . . .

IIIII*THINKING ABOUT THE STORY*

1. Why does Compton hate school?
2. Who is Julia? How can she help Compton?
3. What does Julia suggest that Compton write about?
4. Why does Compton feel that his English teacher, Mr. Childs, does not like him?
5. Why does Compton get angry at Mr. Childs?

IIIII THINKING ABOUT THE ENDING

Julia is left in a very difficult situation at the end of the story. Should she tell the principal that Compton set the fire? She sympathizes with Compton and understands why he is angry, but the fire could have threatened the lives of many people.

Based on what you have learned about Julia and Compton, write an ending in journal form in which Compton and Julia make their decisions.

Homecoming

by Brenda Lane Richardson

As the limousine rounded the corner of the old neighborhood, rap star Al Tee Dee raised a hand to silence Lisa and Mark, his two publicity people. Brooklyn looked just as he remembered it: the streets crowded with restaurants, clothing stores, and furniture shops. However, because it was Christmas, the usually busy streets were quiet.

Al Tee Dee, whose real name was Alvin Thomas Davis, had spent his first 15 years in this neighborhood. He'd worked as a grocery boy at the supermarket that his limo was now passing. Week after week, he'd carried grocery bags for little old ladies who had tipped him a quarter a bag.

Smiling at the memory, he noticed Lisa and Mark were also smiling. They seemed glad that he was happy. It hadn't been easy to get Al to come back here.

He'd been looking forward to having his family and friends visit his new ranch in California. His cousins would have loved the movie theater and huge playhouse he'd built. But Mark had convinced him to come home to Brooklyn instead and serve at the local soup kitchen. It would be a great way to capture public attention for his upcoming world tour.

But Al had other reasons for coming to the soup kitchen. He'd been giving money to the shelter for the last three years—since he'd hit it big. Now, he wanted to put his body where his money was. He didn't want to be the kind of celebrity who is afraid of being around poor people. He wanted to really help.

Al wondered why Mark was wearing a suit to a soup kitchen. Lisa wasn't much better. She looked dressed for a beauty contest. Al had left his jewelry on the jet and had worn his oldest, most worn-out clothes. After all, he'd be serving food to people who couldn't even feed themselves on Christmas Day.

As the limo glided up to the church, the crowd out front cheered. The driver opened the car door, and cold air rushed in. Lisa held out the fur jacket that had been a gift from basketball great Michael Jordan. But Al shook his head. Not today.

Security guards cleared a path through the crowd. Seeing familiar faces from the past, Al reached out to shake hands. Wasn't that Benny? Man, he's seen some hard times, Al thought. He tried to smile despite the pity he felt for his old grade-school buddy. A slender girl shot past the security guards. "Little Alvin," she called. Al recognized her as his former next-door neighbor and smothered her with a hug.

Old friends and neighbors cheered him on, but all Al could think about was how sad they looked. He had to figure out what to do to help them.

Along with the 500 turkey dinners he dished up that day, Al slipped hundred-dollar bills into lots of palms. He signaled each person to keep silent about his gift. If word got around that he was passing out that kind of money, there could be a riot.

Mark and Lisa seemed happy too. Photographers had come from *People*, *Ebony*, and *Jet*, as well as crews from several news and entertainment TV shows. Al was glad he'd done some good, and to top it off, he'd gotten the kind of publicity that money couldn't buy. Maybe he would inspire some other stars to do the same. Right now, though, he needed a break. Calling to Mark and Lisa, he motioned that he was going outside. They signaled for the security guards, but Al insisted on going alone.

With sunglasses on and a knit cap pulled way down over his eyebrows, he slipped out, hoping he wouldn't be recognized. He thrust his hands into the pockets of his sweatshirt and looked just like one more brother fighting the cold. Outside, he was surprised to see so many people hadn't been able to get in. Their faces were not familiar. Once beyond the gate, he stood on the quiet corner and took in some gulps of air. It felt good not to be recognized for a change. This way he could watch others, instead of being the object of everyone else's attention.

When the cold became too much, Al turned to go back inside. The crowd of people waiting out front was angry. Someone had announced that the food had run out. Two young men worked up the crowd. "Al Tee Dee don't care nothing about us," one was saying. "I say we go in there and give Mr. Al Tee Dee what he deserves." Many of the others shouted in agreement.

Al was suddenly frightened. He knew from experience how quickly an angry crowd could turn into a violent mob.

He edged back toward the kitchen door, but there was a new security guard on duty, and he refused to open the gates. "Hey, let me in," Al hissed.

"I told you, no more food today," the guard said.

"But I'm Al Tee Dee," Al whispered.

"Yeah," the man said, smiling at the other guard who worked with him, "and I'm Santa Claus." His voice turned commanding. "Now get out of my face. We've already given you people too much. Why don't you get a job? I've gotta work for mine, even on Christmas Day. Nobody gives *me* hundred-dollar bills."

At the mention of hundred-dollar bills, the crowd began pushing from behind. Al thought about slipping around the side and climbing the fence, but the guards might stop him before he made it to the kitchen. He could pull off his cap and glasses and try to calm the crowd. He didn't have any money left in his wallet, but maybe he could convince them he'd come with the best of intentions. But maybe they'd never give him a chance to explain. Feeling caught between two boulders, Al wondered if there was any hope of getting out safely.

The crowd surged, pushing him back farther and farther from the gate. More people came to see what was happening. There was talk of storming the soup kitchen. Al knew that he had to do something *now*. He took a deep breath and . . .

IIIII THINKING ABOUT THE STORY

1. What has Al done to help his former neighbors?

2. Why does Al feel it is important not to wear fancy clothes to the soup kitchen?

3. Once outside on the street, why does Al enjoy not being recognized?

4. What does the guard mean when he complains that the people had already been given "too much"? Do you think many other people would agree with how he feels? Why?

5. Other than handing out money and donating to the soup kitchen, what other ways might Al help people in his old neighborhood? If you were rich, would you want to help others? How?

IIII▌*THINKING ABOUT THE ENDING*

Al Tee Dee is clearly having conflicting feelings about the people who surround him in front of the food kitchen. On one hand, he wants to help them. On the other hand, he also fears them. What is he thinking as he decides to act? What do you think finally happens?

Use what you have learned about Al Tee Dee's feelings for his old neighborhood and his reasons for returning to write an ending for this story. Describe Al's thoughts and actions and the crowd's reaction to his decision.

Caleb

by Chiori Santiago

I saw the kid standing by the office before the first bell, but I never knew he was going to be my own personal problem. I just glanced in the office like I do every day. My friend Jenny Cabralini works behind the desk, and I like to say "Hi." That's when I saw this kid standing there, and he definitely did not look like he belonged at Mar Vista High.

You could say there are no nerds at Mar Vista. I mean, there are the straight-A, quiet students just like everywhere else, but their parents have the sense to buy their clothes at the mall like the rest of us. So the nerds don't look as nerdy as you might think. Then there are the drama club kids. They love to jump around, attack people with rolled-up binder paper, and make fools of themselves. Then there are the groupie girls, who sit around in the cafeteria at lunchtime talking about rock singers and calling them "poets." They grow out their bangs and try to look sad and mysterious. This is silly because most kids at Mar Vista are healthy, all-American kids. They're not really mysterious at all.

"Caleb!" someone called. I turned around. It was Reese, running up behind me. I forgot about the kid in the office. "Meet us at lunchtime in the courtyard," Reese said. "We have to talk strategy."

I'm a jock. At Mar Vista, that's a hard group to get into, but once you're in, you get more respect than anyone else. I'm in gymnastics, which—after the football team and track—gets the most attention at school. We won a state championship last year. I was on the team, and even though I'm not that tall or buffed or anything, I worked out really hard and it paid off. People really started to notice me. Plus there are only two Asian guys on the team, me and Barry Fong. Barry's more of a nerd. I'm taller than he is, and I'm certainly not a nerd, but you wouldn't believe how many people get us mixed up. Because there aren't that many Asians in the school, they probably think we're all from the same family or something.

Barry's parents were one of the first Asian American families to move out here to the suburbs. Barry's father sells electronics—computers and stuff. They're sixth-generation Chinese American. Barry's never even been to China, but his father went back a few years ago to visit the family village. He had to hire an interpreter because he couldn't speak Chinese.

I can, but I don't like to. Mostly, my parents speak it, and I answer them in English. They're Vietnamese Chinese. They came over almost 20 years ago, before I was born. They love America, but they're always talking about Vietnam. America's been good to them. They started out here on welfare. My dad worked as a janitor, but back in Vietnam he was an engineer. He finally got his engineering license, and now he works for an oil company. We moved to the 'burbs when I was 6.

Sometimes I wonder why we ever moved out here. My parents are old-fashioned, and sometimes that makes life hard for me. They want me to be all-American, but they also want me to be Chinese. They want me to study hard and win gymnastics trophies, but then they get mad when I turn the stereo up loud, or when my friends drop over without an invitation. It's hard to get them to understand that this is how kids are nowadays—American kids. They think we have no respect, but we do. It's just that American kids think of their parents more as friends, which Chinese parents can't understand at all.

When I was a little kid, I was so proud of my dad—the way he worked cleaning floors all day and then went to night school so that he could get a better job and move out here. When we moved, I was in grade school. Even though I was only a kid, I was embarassed because my dad had a Chinese accent, and sometimes my teachers couldn't understand him. Now that I'm older, I think I understand things better. It wasn't easy for my dad to do what he did, but he did it for us.

I made it to homeroom just as the second bell was ringing. Luckily I have a desk at the back of the room. I can jump into it at the last minute.

"Way to go, Caleb," yelled Jeff Wilson, holding up his hand for a five. The homeroom teacher, Ms. Sweeney, looked over my way. As I said, I may wear the same clothes as the other kids, but I don't exactly blend in. There are lots of blonds in this class, and I stand out like a red bean in a bowl of rice. I mean, they're my friends and I'm one of them, but I can never get used to people staring at me.

It's like they don't see me —Caleb— they just see some Asian kid. I overheard some kids talking about the meet with Northside, when we won the state championship. They didn't say, "The guy on the vaults was great!" They said, "Who was that *Chinese* kid?" They weren't impressed that I'd just won the title for the team. They were amazed that a "Chinese" kid made the team. I wanted to walk over to them and say, "Hey, wait a minute, I'm not Chinese, I'm American." I didn't though. I knew they wouldn't get it.

People look at me because I look different from the other kids, but I stand out because I'm a jock, too. Like the way Ms. Sweeney stared at me that morning in homeroom. I thought she was going to give me a tardy detention. They're hard on the jocks because they think we just want to have a good time. Yeah. Even if we weren't forced to keep a B average just to be on the team, I couldn't come home with bad grades. My parents would start screaming in

Chinese and embarass me in front of the whole neighborhood. I'm supposed to be the perfect son. I'm the only son. You wouldn't believe the stress that creates.

So I'm down in my seat, hoping Ms. Sweeney won't really notice me and give me a bad time. But she stopped looking at me. She focused on somebody up front. Uh-oh, I thought.

"I'd like to introduce you to a new student at Mar Vista," she said. She had this smile on her face, and she waved at this kid in the front row. He stood up, looking like he wished he could melt into the wall instead. That's how I'd feel, too. It was the kid who was standing by the office. "This is Timothy Hong Yee, and he'll be with us the rest of the semester," Ms. Sweeney said. "Please make him welcome."

"Yo, Mr. Tim!" Jeff roared from the back of the room, and everyone laughed. "All right," said Ms. Sweeney. She looked at Jeff as if her eyeballs could drill a hole right through his brain. She made the new kid sit down and read the announcements before the bell rang. I began to relax into my seat.

"Caleb." I froze. I was just about to do a perfect scissor split over the chair-desk when Ms. Sweeney's voice broke my focus. I sat down hard on the desk top. Here we go, I thought.

"Caleb, come here a moment," she said with a smile. "I thought you'd be the perfect person to help Timothy here." She was standing with one hand on the kid's shoulder. "I mean, I'm sure you know what it's like to be a newcomer."

No, I don't, I'm thinking. I was born here, just like everybody else in this class. I take a good look at the new kid. Now this, I think, is what gives Asians a bad name. Coke-bottle glasses. Pants that didn't reach his ankles. Loafers. A white shirt buttoned up to the neck. A haircut that went out of style in the '60s. No, I thought, we have nothing in common.

"Now, Timothy is from Taiwan. You speak Chinese, don't you, Caleb?" Ms. Sweeney asked. "I think it would be so helpful for Timothy to have someone to show him around."

"I come to better English," Timothy said to her. "No Chinese." He stared at me through those glasses. Maybe I looked weird to him, too.

What could I say? One thing I've learned: Americans think all Asians are the same. They think a Taiwanese Chinese speaks the same language as a Vietnamese Chinese. They don't. A lot of the words are totally different. Plus, I'm a Vietnamese Chinese born in the good old U.S.A. When I try talking to my relatives in Chinese, they laugh at my accent.

"Yeah, OK, Ms. Sweeney," I said. "But right now, I've got to run. I'm late." I nodded at Timothy, and he followed me out of homeroom. I felt as if we were back in the second grade.

The hallway was empty. Timothy was staring at me again. He didn't look shy or scared. He looked kind of mad. Maybe he doesn't like this setup any more than I do, I thought. "Show me the paper," I said in Chinese. I felt kind of stupid, because I didn't know the words for *class list*. They didn't come up with my parents.

"Speak English," Timothy said, handing me the list.

"OK. Look, your first class is in the C Building, that way." I pointed. "Then you walk across the courtyard to the Science Center, there. You're there for two periods. I'm busy at lunchtime, so you're on your own. But I'll meet you here after school to show you where the bus stops. You know which bus you need, right? You understand?" I patted him on the arm.

"I know about the bus," Timothy said. He stood there stiffly, his arms at his sides. He reminded me of someone. My father, I thought. My dad, who was always proud, even when he worked as a janitor. My dad had that look when he was learning English or when he went off to work after studying for his license all night. It was the Chinese warrior look, I used to think. As if no matter what happened, he was going to win.

"OK. Well. Tim. Good luck, OK? See ya. That way." I almost patted him on the shoulder, but then I remembered that he might take it as an insult. I pointed one more time. He walked off. He looked like a duck in those pants. Watching him, I was glad I wouldn't have to hang around with him the rest of the day.

The guys ragged me at lunchtime. "Wow, check out the baby sitter for Charlie Chinaman," said Reese.

"Shut up," I said. I knew he was just kidding. We've known each other for years, and Reese, Taylor, and Smitty think they can joke like that because we're buddies. Usually they can, but, I don't know, I just felt weird.

"Come on, Caleb, we weren't talking about you," Taylor said. "You're no Chinaman."

"Yeah, yeah, all right," I said. "So what's the game plan? I want that tournament, man. I mean, this year, that medal is *mine*." I didn't want to think about old geeky Timothy. I wanted to leave him far behind. I couldn't help wondering though—maybe if I wasn't born here, I'd be a Chinaman, too. But I *was* born here. I belong here. I like cheeseburgers better than *chow fun.* I like metal music and skateboard movies. I'm an American, you know. I'd be a foreigner in China.

"Hey, Caleb, your boy is looking for you," said Reese. I looked across the courtyard. I could see Timothy standing there, looking around. He looked toward me and I turned away, as if I didn't see him. I felt kind of bad, but what was I supposed to do? Then I thought about the Chinese warrior. What would my father do if someone called him a Chinaman?

"Here comes Mr. Tim Tong," Reese laughed, poking me.

That was it. I had to set things straight. I turned to face Reese and said . . .

▮▮▮▮ THINKING ABOUT THE STORY

1. How does Caleb feel about Mar Vista High? Give evidence from the story.

2. Given that he performs on the gymnastics team, why does Caleb feel uncomfortable when people stare at him?

3. Why does Caleb think Timothy "gives Asians a bad name"?

4. What is Caleb's relationship with Reese, Taylor, and Smitty?

5. Why is Caleb upset by the comments they make about Timothy?

6. Why doesn't Caleb feel a kinship with Timothy, as they're both Chinese?

Caleb has found a comfortable place for himself at Mar Vista High. Now he has to help a newcomer with whom he has little in common except that they are both of Chinese descent. Is this enough to help the two form a friendship? Should Caleb befriend Timothy, or would Timothy be better off paired with another student?

Using what you know about Caleb, write an ending that shows the decision you think he would make.